CHTHONIC MATTER

A DARK FICTION QUARTERLY

Edited by

C. M. Muller

Summer 2024 (Volume 2, Issue 2)

CONTENTS

CORVID SUMMER

Tom Johnstone

It was the summer the ravens began leaving the Tower when Howard first met Rowan Avery. Their gradual departure didn't signal some grand national catastrophe, nothing worse than the usual slow-dripping slop of day-to-day horror that passed for normality nowadays. It was surprising they hadn't flown the stony coop with its four spike-domed turrets years ago. Perhaps the apocalypse was too sluggish for them, so that like frogs immersed in water heated by imperceptible degrees until boiled alive, they only fulfilled the ancient prophecy attached to them once the damage was irreversible.

Howard wasn't to find out the real reason for their absence until the following autumn, when he visited the Tower in search of Rowan.

It was Alice Rook who introduced them. She first mentioned Rowan during a discussion of the nature of fictional characters and whether it was necessary to plot a timeline of their personal development. Howard swore by the method, but Alice disagreed, citing her friend Rowan as an example of someone who couldn't be reduced to a chronological shopping list of experiences.

"But then she's not like most people," Alice said. "She's part raven for a start."

Alice Rook was her stage name anyway, and the one she told him at the party where they met. No one seemed to know who she was before she adopted this persona and at the time Howard himself had little curiosity regarding her original self. With her dyed-pink hair and talk of the one-woman show she was working on, he initially wrote her off in the summary knee-jerk way he often did as just another one of Brighton's perennial army of Bohemians, whose presence made his stomach churn and his teeth grind with a peculiar, irritated embarrassment, partly at his own pretensions. He was a writer after all, so he too was part of that battalion, but he didn't like to think of himself that way.

Perhaps that was why, despite his initial skepticism about her talents, there was something endearing about her. Maybe it was the sardonic estuary drawl with which she called herself "a creative," and the strange expression, somewhere between a scowl and a smirk, that accompanied this declaration. There wasn't a word in the English language that could really describe it adequately. Maybe he should invent one: s*mowk* or *skirl*. It certainly wasn't a smile.

Her pale blue eyes regarded him as he stood there, lost for words, but then he always thought himself better at writing them than uttering them aloud.

"What?" she said.

"It's just that word—*creative*."

"What's wrong with it?"

"Oh nothing. Not as an adjective anyway. You just used it as a noun."

"Did I? Oh. Annoying when people do that, isn't it?"

She broke into a smile.

He didn't know if it was the rarity of it, but it made him catch his breath. Eventually, after they'd talked for a while, she moved on, circulating through the party, leaving him standing alone cradling his drink self-consciously. He wasn't actually on his own of course. The room was packed full of people, but he suddenly found it impossible to concentrate on anything anyone said to him, too preoccupied by the elfin, pink-haired figure now apparently reveling in the attentions of a goatee-bearded man with flowing hair and expansive, ostentatious laugh. Just the kind of guy who really got up Howard's nose. He watched them for a while. Stung by her cackling mirth at something the goatee man whispered into her almost pointed ear, his expression lewd and intimate, he could bear it no longer and slipped out quietly. No one would miss him.

After a while, the self pity wore off, but he sought her out on social media and eventually they ran into each other again.

By now her one-woman show had taken on a different form, she said, and was to be on-screen only. This was partly out of necessity, for the same reasons that the event that saw their second encounter was a barbecue limited to six people. Theaters and other performance venues were all closed now and the only possible outlet for her performance art was a virtual one. Her hair was now midnight black. He also noticed with a sinking, knotted feeling in his stomach that Goatee Man was one of the other select few invited.

"You'll have to ask Rowan about that," said Alice, when he queried her change of hair color.

"Who's she?"

"A friend of mine. I'll introduce you if you're good."

Her face broke into the puckish smile that so beguiled him when she saw him looking around the garden at the other four guests in search of Alice's mysterious friend, as if she might be concealed by the smoke from the charcoal.

"She's not here, you idiot." She laughed. "Well, she is . . . in a sense."

"I thought you were going to introduce us."

"Not now. Another time."

"I look forward to it."

"Freak."

She walked off. He drank too much and stayed until it got dark. As the evening grew colder, the party moved inside, to a room dominated by a pool table. Alice and Goatee Man played, she endearingly inept, he increasingly tactile in his attempts to instruct her in the finer points of the game. Howard felt sick, his vision mainly blurred, but too sharply focused on certain things. Perhaps it was inebriation, but the sight of her ears tapering between gaps in her feathery hair almost made him want to weep. Goatee Man guided Alice's hands on the cue from behind, his bulk dwarfing her, his groin pressing against her back. To Howard's horror, the couple hosting the barbecue smirked at each other meaningfully, as if tacitly blessing the forthcoming union.

"What about physical distancing?" said Howard, his voice a shrill and querulous squawk—but his Cassandra-cry was ignored, if not derided.

After he'd beaten her at pool, Goatee Man sat with Alice outside, conversing intimately, one of his huge hands brushing her knee. Howard could almost smell his pheromones over the smoldering embers and incinerated food aromas of the barbecue. With a knowing glance their way, the host couple suggested the remaining guests move back inside.

"Anyone for another game?"

Howard hesitated. He would rather take a belt-sander to his eyes than watch any more of what might unfold between Alice and Goatee Man. The host couple stared at him pointedly as they made for the pool room. Howard gave his excuses and left. When he got home, he lay there trying to read, his eyes struggling to focus on the book, unable to put one word after another. The mist of tears didn't help. Even rejection letters hurt less than this.

It was just tiredness, he decided the following day. That must be the reason she'd got to him so much; that, and the strangely circumscribed world he now lived in. He would forget about her. She was not unattractive, he had to admit, with her wasp-waist and wasp-tongue, but nothing to get so worked up about.

Yet when he tried to work on his latest book, he found himself checking Facebook—and there she was, all over it. Pretty soon her digital footprint spread over him like a pattern of bruises. Messenger pinged. It was Alice Rook, with a video of her one-woman show.

I told you I'd introduce you to Rowan, said the accompanying message.

What he saw was a vlog of sorts, but not the kind of thing Zoella was putting out. The pale-blue eyes were Alice's. The strange, lost look in them was perhaps someone else's. Her raven-black hair had faded to a mellower cinnamon color, he noticed. Hair dye was obviously hard to come by in these strange times.

"Let me introduce myself," Alice intoned in a faint Yorkshire accent. "My name is Rowan Avery. Welcome to my 'rona aviary. Think of me as your spiritual personal trainer . . . "

He watched, rapt, as she continued her spiel, going into what appeared to be the instructions for some kind of recipe, but the ingredients on display weren't exactly edible: Datura, Belladonna, Mandragora, Papaver . . . so the narration solemnly announced. Thin, pale hands tossed in these items with twitching, febrile motions. Howard almost dropped his device when the image appeared to glitch, then Alice's face was replaced by a black beaked one, the eyes two vast shining dinner plates, dark pools of nothingness. Another glitchy jump-cut and the face was Alice's again, or Rowan's to be exact. There was a difference, for where Alice's smile delighted him, Rowan's sphinxlike glacial grin terrified him, and something in her tone of voice reminded him of the kind of Second World War propaganda posters that demanded whether or not your journey was necessary or cautioned that loose lips sank ships. It seemed to fit with the tense, judgmental atmosphere of the halfheartedly locked-down land.

Later she messaged him again to ask if he'd watched it.

What did you think? I'm hoping it'll go viral.

It's good. Are you hoping to become a social media influenza?

That's terrible. You really are a freak. What did you really think?

It's great. I loved it—just the sort of weird shit I like. Made me think of the Celtic goddess, Morrigan.

Creep.

No, I mean it.

Well, I meant: How did you know my mother's maiden name was Morrison, creep?

I didn't know, but it's serendipitous. Anyway, it's not spelled like that—it's Mór-Rioghain, the phantom queen, who hangs around battlefields in the guise of a crow. She encourages warriors to carry out brave deeds, strikes fear into their enemies and washes the blood-stained clothes of those fated to die—or so wicca-pedia tells me.

Nice. Very drole. So you're not stalking me then.

No.

Good. 'Serendipitous' indeed. Knobhead! So I suppose you think it's loveably 'quirky'.

What?

The video, you plonker.

Oh God, no, not that, thank goodness.

Did you like the mask?

What mask?

Oh, ha ha!

Where did you find it?

In an antique shop in the Laines. It's a genuine, fourteenth century plague doctor mask.

Really? I hope you sanitized it.

She didn't answer. He sat there listening out for the ping of the messenger app, waiting for her profile picture to replace the grey tick, which would indicate she had *read* the message at least. Eventually, he returned to what he was supposed to be doing, a novel already promised to a publisher and long overdue, but his attempts to make progress with it were listless at best. He was sickening for something, or rather someone, craving the scraps of playful insults Alice tossed his way. He was even growing confident enough to throw some of his own back at her.

But the words he added to the holy edifice of his book seemed empty shells, shambling along like the zombie economy barely reanimated by lackluster fiscal stimulus, preserving it in aspic while caution suspended the human association upon which the novel coronavirus thrived. Weeks later, its unfinished edifice reminded him of the abandoned building projects on the edge of town, girded by scaffolding showing signs of corrosion, walls crenellated by unfinished brickwork, cranes standing idly by, sentinels turning a blind eye to stagnation.

That was a nice image, but it didn't actually reflect the truth: of construction workers forced into close proximity to carry on working despite the risk of infection for fear of being out of a job, out of pocket and out on the streets in these uncertain times. The building sites on the edge of town still ground on, even if the cafes and pubs they would eventually house might never open.

He decided he'd use the image anyway in the short story he was working on, as a displacement activity from the neglected novel. It concerned a performance artist called Rose Atwater—the short story that is, not the novel. Howard struggled to remember what *that* was about! The story was a bit on the nose—the woman in it was a blue-haired, sharp-tongued manic pixie dream-girl who had an ice-blonde alter ego called Ava Rooney. The incomplete buildings and rusting scaffolding poles would make a fitting image for the post-apocalyptic landscape he was trying to evoke. He couldn't help wondering if he was being as cavalier with his heroine as he was with the economic situation. It occurred to him he didn't even know what she did for a living, with the result that he wrote about her as if she financed her creative projects with a trust fund or something. Truth was an important aspect of his own fiction writing, up to a point. Perhaps he needed to carry out closer observation of her real-life counterpart. He didn't have her number, but one afternoon his mouse lingered too long on the video call icon on her messenger feed the way a bird of prey might hover over its target. Suddenly it swooped down, virtually at least, and he was dismayed to see the call was ringing. Before he worked out how to stop it, her face glowered back at him.

"What do *you* want?" her tinny voice snapped.

"Nice to see you too! In fact it was an accident, but seeing as you're here, how are things?"

"I'm busy. Look, this is a bit intrusive. I'm working on my vlog at the moment."

"That was what I wanted to ask you about. How's it going with Ava?"

" 'Ava?' "

"Er . . . I meant Rowan."

"Nightmare. Maybe you could help me, I suppose."

That rather grudging offer set the pattern for their relationship. His abject eagerness to comply made him feel as if she was the one doing him a favor, which in a sense she was. The truth was, he would have crawled through broken glass to do her bidding. Not that that was required. She only wanted him to hold a camera and record her, in the persona of Rowan, running some kind of lock-down exercise class for the dead in the local cemetery, the idea behind her latest mock-vlog.

"This Covid malarkey has turned you lot into a right bunch of layabouts," she hectored the gravestones in a more exaggerated Yorkshire accent than on the previous blog, pronouncing the name of the disease *Caw-vid.* "But don't worry . . . Rowan Avery'll soon lick you into shape!"

The kinds of movements this macabre boot camp involved were frenetic and birdlike, and for some of the takes she donned the plague doctor mask, whose beak jerked hither and thither and pecked at the air. Her costume was made of black and tight-fitting lycra, which he thought looked uncomfortable in the heat. Maybe the itchiness of the artificial fabric was the reason she kept scratching at her arm between shots.

When she caught him looking, she gave him a hard stare.

"What are you perving at?" she demanded, still in character he guessed from the accent, though sometimes it was hard to tell Alice and Rowan apart.

"I can't *help* looking at you!" he protested, shrill enough to wake the dead, which seemed to be the object of the exercise in any case. "If I'm filming you, I mean," he added quickly.

"Oh, yes, I suppose so. Well, I think we'll call it a wrap now. It's getting too dark to film now anyway."

They headed towards the gates. Howard glanced behind him apprehensively. He could hear faint sounds behind him, probably small animals, he guessed, becoming more active as dusk descended upon the cemetery—now deserted apart from him and Alice, and whatever was moving under cover of the sprawling euonymus and spiked yew hedges, whose dark foliage provided ample concealment for their shuffling. Come to think of it, some of the noises sounded like the scrape of stone slabs moving.

"Bollocks," Alice said. "The gate's locked."

"Oh," said Howard. "Well, we could climb over. Here—let me give you a bunk-up."

She slapped his proffered hand away.

"In your dreams, sunshine. Don't even think about it. Keep your physical distance. I've got a plan."

Whatever it was seemed to involve her tapping out a rhythm on her smartphone. Howard's heart sank when he saw the secret smile up-lit by the device's blue light. Her text and her prayers had been answered. Before long, an all-too-familiar goatee-bearded figure swaggered toward the gate, the new arrival about as welcome as a cup of cold sick as far as Howard was concerned.

"Not that blow-hard," he muttered. "I *thought* there was a whiff of testosterone in the air . . . "

"Ooh, not half," Alice purred. "You shouldn't be so mean about him, Howard," she added tartly. "He might seem really confident on the surface, but underneath it he's very sensitive and insecure."

As Goatee Man grinned broadly through the bars imprisoning them, brandishing a set of keys like those of a gaoler, Howard wished the man could be sensitive and insecure on the surface too, but despite his resentment at the means of their deliverance, he was relieved at this rescue, as the scuffling, scraping sounds behind them were growing louder and closer at their heels, provoking visions in him of a *danse macabre* of crumbling limbs answering Rowan's call to some spectral boot camp.

"See? I told you I worked in the parks department," Goatee Man said with a smirk, jangling the metallic cluster in his meaty fist, then finding the key that fitted the padlock. "We also cover cemeteries," he added unnecessarily.

"My hero," Alice said with a smirk as he opened the gate.

Goatee Man smiled with uncharacteristic modesty as he ushered her outside, barely acknowledging Howard.

"You two *have* met, haven't you?" she asked, and the two grunted in confirmation. "You know what? I could murder a pint after that ordeal." She looked longingly at a pub nearby, and Howard wondered self-pityingly if the "ordeal" referred to their temporary incarceration in the cemetery or of having to endure his own company in order to gain the footage she required. Hardly the former, as she seemed quite at home among the dead.

"Still," she added, "I don't suppose at this hour we'll be able to get a table."

"It's all right," said Goatee Man, running a hand through his black ponytail. "I booked one."

"Smooth," said Alice, still scratching at her arm.

"For two. I didn't know there was anyone else with you."

How convenient, thought Howard, feeling not so much like a gooseberry but as if he'd swallowed an entire such bush, thorns and all. He watched as they disappeared inside the strangely forlorn-looking drinking establishment, now modified with a welter of Covid warning signs and arrows and other ritual protection marks. She and Goatee Man were surgically masked, arm in arm, with her leaning into him.

"So much for physical distancing," he muttered, recalling the way she'd reprimanded him when he got too close.

Imagining Alice melting in Goatee Man's arms was more than he could bear, so he consoled himself with Rowan. Not literally, of course; rather, with his conception of her . . . He couldn't imagine Alice's *alter ego* giving the brute anything other than short shrift. Once home, he resumed work on his short story with frantic gusto, giving his version, Ava Rooney, all the characteristics of a martinet, a kind of traffic warden of the soul. When he'd finished, it was getting light and he could hear birdsong. He tried not to think of Alice and the kind of all-nighter he suspected she might have pulled. He fell into an exhausted sleep, barely even remembering what he'd written.

He awoke to the sound of his phone bleating with the video messenger ringtone—and, when he answered it, to Alice spitting feathers from a strangely bird-like face. It was three o'clock in the afternoon.

"What have you done, Howard?"

"What do you mean? And why are you wearing that plague doctor mask?"

"This is no time for facetiousness, Howard. Did *you* ring the council misconduct hotline?"

The way her head moved, it looked as if she was trying to peck at him through the screen.

"Alice, I've no idea what you're talking about."

"Oh, don't you? Well, I hope you're satisfied. Malcolm's probably going to lose his job now because of what you've done. And how's he going to find another in the current . . . "

He racked his brain for what he could have done, and who Malcolm was for that matter. Of course: Goatee Man. Howard had never bothered to ask for his name. But that still begged the question of what he'd done.

" . . . weren't for him, we'd still be stuck in there. Or maybe that's what you wanted. Hoping for a quick fumble in the dark, were you, Howard? Well, you can forget about that!"

It couldn't be the plague doctor mask, because the beak was opening and shutting as she spoke and the eyes were her own pale blue ones, not black reflective dinner plates. Maybe it was one of those video effects you could superimpose over your face. She'd tried some of these out on him during one of their previous video calls. He wondered that she didn't notice the transformation, which must be visible on-screen. That was the thing with these calls. You couldn't help looking at your own face, checking your appearance from time to time.

"Well? What have you got to say for yourself, Howard? Howard, are you listening to me?"

He was that all right. He was all ears. But as for what to say, it was hard to concentrate with that corvid head rapping out her words.

"I've been asleep all day, so how could I have rung this hotline?" His voice was becoming heated, angry. "I didn't even know there was one, but even if I did, I couldn't have called it in my sleep, could I?"

"Oh, Howard," she said, the cerulean-blue eyes in the bird-face looking incongruously amused, even tender, at his outburst. "This is a new assertive side of you I never knew you had. What were you doing all night that you slept in so late then?"

The softening of her tone, bordering on the salacious, sounded weird coming from the ridged black beak, making him defensive.

"If you must know, I was writing."

"No need to be huffy. I wasn't suggesting anything indecent. What were you writing, Howard?"

Flattered as he was by her mild interest in his work, he was unable to come up with anything.

"I can't actually remember what I was writing about."

"Oh. Well, maybe it isn't worth remembering then."

She looked as if she was about to end the call and he wondered if he would see fingers or feathers moving toward the screen. Stung by her dismissive tone, and genuinely curious to see the results of his nocturnal labors, he opened his laptop.

"Hang on . . . let me have a look."

"Well, hurry up then. I haven't got all day."

The beak widened in a stark yawn. Howard opened the Word document, gazed at his handiwork, and began to read it out aloud.

"Ava Rooney stared at the hulking specimen of masculinity outside the cemetery gate. Behind her, the Dance of the Dead was getting under way.

" 'Well, Mr. Sideburns,' she snapped imperiously through the raven's mask that was now her true face, 'I suppose you think you've come to rescue me from this place and sweep me off my feet. Well, think again. I'm not going anywhere. I've got a work-out to lead. These cadavers need my guidance to get themselves in shape for the afterlife. They've got bloated over lock-down, stuck in their boxes. I can't let them stew in their own juices, can I?'

"Mr. Sideburns waved his keys impotently.

" 'Is that council property you're misusing? I think you'll find that's a breach of your contract.'

"She dug in her pocket for her phone and began tapping out a number on the touch-screen with woodpecker fingers, oblivious to his pleas for clemency.

" 'Hello, is this the Council Misconduct Hotline? I've got a complaint . . . ' "

Howard broke off to gauge her reaction. But the bird-face's expression was somewhat unreadable, the beak ominously still. Eventually, she spoke.

"So this Ava Rooney is supposed to be me, is she?"

"Well, Rowan," he admitted. "Look, Alice, I don't even remember writing—"

"You've done okay. Yes, you seem to get it. But Howard, if you're going to publish this, I want a co-credit, okay?"

He nodded. Before he had a chance to ask if she wanted it under the name Alice Rook or Rowan Avery, she was gone.

And that was the last he saw or heard from her, on social media or anywhere else.

For weeks afterwards, the town was somewhat preoccupied with news reports of the suspected desecration of graves in the cemetery where they'd been filming, accompanied by rumors that the tombs had been disturbed from within rather than without. Not to mention the even wilder stories of corpses attempting jerky burpees, frenetic star jumps, and ill-advised planks, shedding decomposing limbs in the process, attracting hordes of carrion crows.

Howard was keen to discuss these matters with Alice, also check which name she wanted on the byline, but she wasn't replying to his messages. Come to that, she seemed to have disappeared from Facebook, something her previous ubiquity there cast in sharp relief. He began to worry that her annoyance at his fictional appropriation was the explanation for her breaking off communication with him.

When no reply was forthcoming, he began to search for her in cemeteries and other open spaces where ravens and other corvids could be found, wondering if the strange transformation to her face during that last video call was not in fact an effect but the beginning of a more total, physical metamorphosis. Finally, he donned a surgical mask and bought a one-way ticket to London, where he stayed in a hotel until his funds ran out. Every day, he went to the Tower.

He got talking to one of the Beefeaters, who looked a little odd with his face shield and mask sandwiched between his garlanded black hat and his neck-ruffed, heraldic, red tunic resplendent with the royal coat of arms. He was friendly enough, but he wouldn't let Howard in to see the Raven Master.

"Not many left," he said, looking dubiously at Howard's unshaven face and crumpled, unwashed clothes.

"Really? Why not?"

"Getting bored, I suppose, because the Tower's closed to the public. Covid, see? So, no visitors. Nothing to keep them here now."

"You haven't seen one that's a bit *unusual* now, have you?" Howard hissed eagerly through his snot- and spittle-soiled mask, and he moved closer to whisper something into the Beefeater's ear, so the usually stoical giant almost flinched away at the smell of destitution and desperation, not to mention the potential viral load the vagrant was packing.

The Beefeater shook his head, tight-lipped, his face closing like a portcullis, leaving Howard to return to his grimy sleeping bag in an alley nearby, which offered a good view of the Tower. There he lay, shivering and watching to see if any ravens flew out. If he was lucky, he might be able to entice one over with some scraps of food, close enough to get a good look at the eyes, see if one of them was his lost phantom queen.

As he watched the stranger shamble away disconsolately, the Beefeater, whose name was Cyril, shook his head again as he thought of the frantically whispered enquiry, wondering if he'd heard it correctly. The man obviously hadn't seen that many ravens. Cyril didn't know that much about them himself, but he was certain of one thing. He'd never heard of any with pale-blue eyes.

TOM JOHNSTONE is a senior gardener with Brighton and Hove City Council, whose short stories sometimes grow into longer works when he uses too much fertilizer. His fiction has appeared in various publications, including *Black Static, Nightscript, Body Shocks, The Ghosts and Scholars Book of Folk Horror, Terror Tales of the Home Counties, Come October, Supernatural Tales* and *Best Horror of the Year,* as well as the collections *Last Stop Wellsbourne,* originally published by Omnium Gatherum Books, and *Let Your Hinged Jaw Do the Talking,* from Alchemy Press. His other accomplishments include an English and Drama degree from Exeter University and a LANTRA certificate in the use of a John Deere ride-on lawnmower. More information at tomjohnstone.wordpress.com.

EXIT WOUND

Phoebe Murphy

I've seen one person turn inside out since it started two years ago. It was at a shopping center ten minutes from my house. It was a woman, heavily pregnant, and I was four customers behind her in line at a coffee kiosk. Because of the line, I couldn't see her expression when she realized what was about to occur, but this is how I imagined it:

She's tired, the baby is taking its toll. She strokes her belly with one hand. She goes to wipe the exhaustion from her eyes with the other, and it comes away bloody. She understands what is about to happen. That's how I imagined it.

"Get back!" she told us. We obeyed.

The scarlet flower of skin and muscle hadn't even finished bursting from her mouth before several people were on their phones, calling for cleanup. Streams of blood ran down her body, spreading into a black pool at her feet before she collapsed. She did not scream; there was no time for her to scream. The fetid stench of blood and feces rolled off her flesh in waves. The articles I had read about people turning did nothing to prepare me for the real thing. And yet, the sight of the woman as she revealed herself to us—of pink flesh turning and peeling away—tugged at the edges of my vision and urged me to stay.

When I finally willed myself to go home, it was on the local news that the woman's baby had actually survived. The cleanup crew found it in the ruins of her body and took it to the hospital. It was a triumph—new life in the wake of destruction.

Until later that night, when they reported that the infant had turned as well, in the strong and gentle arms of a NICU nurse. No one was impervious. It happened at random. A sudden and gruesome death loomed over us all.

MY HUSBAND JOHN came home as I was making dinner and told me how one of the interns at his advertising agency, a young thing named Gemma, turned in the break room during lunch. Three people threw up, he said, two men and one woman. He sounded apologetic as he went on between bites of catfish about what a bright and diligent girl she was. How rough the cleanup crew was with her body. Didn't even bother with the stain. That's against procedure, you know.

He said, "You have to be brave to come into work these days."

He wanted me to validate him—*You* are *brave, honey*—but I said nothing. He'd seen four people turn, to my one. I thought that had something to do with it.

I collected his dirty plate, then mine, and went to the sink to scrub them clean. We had a dishwasher, but I liked to do them by hand.

John waved his hand, as if clearing my silence from the room, and changed the subject. "I'm going to D.C. tomorrow," he said. "Big conference. You know the deal." He always waited until the night before to tell me.

"Flying?" I asked.

"Yeah."

These days you had to sign a waiver to get on a plane, in the event both pilots turned. It hadn't happened yet, but in time it would.

"Okay," I said.

THE NEXT MORNING, a Friday, we woke up at five o'clock. John opened the blinds in the kitchen and turned on the kettle for coffee. I sat at the table and warmed my hands on my mug as he rushed around, taking inventory.

Briefcase. Got it.

Suitcase. By the door.

Carry-on. Over there.

Okay, thank you. Don't want to be behind schedule. Got everything? Think so. I'll be back Saturday night. Late.

"And remember," I said. "If it happens—"

"Don't fight it. It just makes it worse." It had become a

motto of sorts.

John counted his luggage a final time, then hoisted it up, kissed me on the cheek, and went out the door.

Whenever he went on one of his trips, I made sure to take something out of his bags at the last minute. Nothing too important. Maybe one sock out of a pair. Maybe a book he told me he wanted to read on the plane. He always brought more than one.

This time, it was the empty metal water bottle he planned to fill up after getting through security. I knew he would complain about the overpriced water on the other side.

"You forgot this," I would say when he came home.

SATURDAY WAS THE second day of John's absence. He'd sent a text at eight—*morning, love you*—to which I had not yet responded. Instead, I left my phone plugged in on the nightstand next to the bottle I'd taken out of his carry-on. I went downstairs to my desk and opened my laptop to a familiar document.

As a freelance editor, I left the house much less frequently than John. I used to be jealous he got to go out more than me. Now it was a blessing to stay indoors, if you were able to.

I'd had many clients in all flavors over the years—from clipped, economical articles to books like thick mortar that pushed me into a fog for weeks at a time. This particular manuscript was a young adult novel about a teenage boy getting transported away to a strange planet of cosmic monarchies and intergalactic warfare. It wasn't particularly original, but any piece not having to do with the turning was a welcome respite. Most of all, though, I relished the influence I had, the invisible privilege of change.

An hour passed editing. Then two. I was almost ready to take a break when the doorbell rang, long and insistent. More of a whine than the intended ring, really, because it was broken and neither John nor I cared to have it fixed.

I closed my laptop and went to the door, apprehensive. I wasn't expecting anyone. We rarely had guests anymore. Maybe it was a salesperson or a Jehovah's Witness, or someone looking for John who was unaware he was on a business trip. But when I looked through the peephole, it wasn't any of those. It was Alexandra.

We'd met in high school, sophomore year. She was a transfer student. The memory I had of her, as she turned around to introduce herself in our American Lit class, often closed itself around me like a fist. Open smile, the color of a salmon sunrise. Coarse black hair down to her chest. Eyes like broken amber glass shrouded by lashes so long and dark I wanted to pluck them out and have them for myself. I was old enough then to know what I wanted.

Shaking, I fumbled with the deadbolt and threw the door open. And there she was, trembling, with blood—so much blood—all down the front of her white blouse, on her arms, in her hair, some dried, some still glistening wet.

"Alexandra?" She reached for my hand, and I took a step back. "What happened to you?"

"It's Graham," she pleaded. There were lines on her face where tears had washed away blood. "Anna, he's dead."

I felt the corner of my mouth twitch. Graham, dead. The reason I hadn't seen Alexandra in five years. She erased her online presence after they got together. Said she didn't believe in such things anymore. Bullshit. I knew better than that. He was the one who whisked her away to Louisiana on a week's notice. He was the one who changed her phone number after they moved.

"He turned?" I asked.

"We were just going to breakfast," she said, looking at her hands as they clutched the air in front of her. "I was driving. And then he just went. Right next to me. There was so much blood. I didn't know what to do. I put him in the trunk and—"

I looked over her shoulder. A white Mercedes, streaked with brown, was parked outside my house. Likely bought by Graham with money he didn't have.

"You drove all the way from Blanchard with him in the trunk?" I asked. I lived in Dallas. "You didn't call for cleanup?"

"I didn't know what to do," she repeated. "I wasn't ready."

"We need to go to a facility," I said. "Now."

Alexandra surrendered and stepped away from the threshold. I came out onto the porch and locked the door behind me, looking stoically ahead as I passed her on the way to the Mercedes. Her high heels clicked in careful intervals behind me. Once we got to the car, I held my hand out for the keys.

"Let me drive," I said. "I know where the closest one is."

She turned over the keys. The fob was rusted with blood that flaked off under my fingers. I told her to get in the car, and she did. My thumb hovered over the trunk release button.

"Are you getting in?" Alexandra called from inside the car.

"Give me a second," I said, and I only hesitated a moment longer before I pressed the button.

The trunk clicked open, and I was met with a jumble of leaking flesh that had stained the entire space red. The smell of metallic rot rose off of it, as real and tactile as smoke. Tufts of sandy hair protruded from one end of the bloody mass, along with an inch of jawbone embedded in the folds. Graham's body struck me as uglier somehow, more grotesque than the woman at the mall. I saw beauty in the way she had unfurled intimately before me. Graham had collapsed in on himself, closed himself off, a tumor.

Not a single thing stirred in me. Certainly not grief. But not the rush of deliverance I was expecting, either. I slammed the trunk closed and got in the driver's seat.

Alexandra was sitting in the back, and there was a towel draped over the passenger seat. If its job was to cover up Graham's blood, it wasn't doing a very good job.

"We're going," I said as I pulled the car away from the house.

The drive to the cleanup facility was only ten minutes, but the silence made it feel twice as long. Alexandra kept her gaze fixed out the window with an unsettling constancy, as if it was a game not to meet my eyes in the rearview mirror. She occasionally let her head tip forward, so it rested against the glass and jumped slightly when I hit a disturbance in the road. Combinations of words to fill the gap formed on my tongue, then dissolved as quickly as they came.

Finally, Alexandra spoke.

"I've missed you," she said, still staring out the window.

I had long believed I could hear her life in her voice when she talked. I heard her childhood, growing up in a land where fields ran for acres in every direction. I heard the triumph and defeat of debate tournaments won and tests failed. The nervous excitement of possibility when we attended college together. I heard the darkness of summer months, when she refused to wear shorts above the knee and I stole glimpses of her unscrewing the blades on pencil sharpeners when she thought no one was watching. Don't think I didn't notice such things.

But what now? What did I hear in the vast canyon of her voice that opened before me, in my five years' absence from her life? Nothing. Nothing at all.

A moment passed. Her hair glinted in the mirror. It was shoulder-length now, and dyed platinum blonde. It looked so much better long and dark. I tightened my grip on the wheel.

"I missed you too," I said.

WE ARRIVED AT the cleanup facility just as one of their vans was leaving, no doubt in response to a call. It left quickly and quietly. The vans had no need for sirens or flashing lights—they existed only to pick up after death, not alter the course of it. The facility itself had once been an auto repair shop that went out of business three years ago, though was never demolished. When people started turning, they repurposed it.

I pulled up to the front of it where an employee in a white hazmat suit was standing with a clipboard. I got out of the car and motioned to him.

"We have one," I said, and he hurried over. I opened the trunk so he could see. He clicked his pen.

"Name?" he asked.

"Alexandra Harris," Alexandra said as she emerged from the back seat.

"Relation to the deceased?"

"My husband."

The man scribbled on his clipboard, then extracted several more pieces of information from her before asking me for the car keys. I handed them over.

"We have it under control from here." He turned to Alexandra. "Please, take as long as you need in the bathroom. We have spare clothes inside, and there's a counselor in the building."

THE SINGLE-PERSON bathroom was large and very nice, and they had several of them. The floor was spotless white tile, the wallpaper an ivory floral, blossoms in gold leaf sprouting at regular intervals across its surface. Against the wall, there was a rack of donated clothes with a sign that said, *Clean. Take what you need.* I had donated clothes here before. There was even a shower in the corner, the good kind with a frosted glass door. All these purposeful, comforting luxuries.

We stepped in and locked the shower door. Alexandra had done a good job keeping her composure—she had always been great at that. But I was also familiar with her breathing, and I recognized the pattern that meant everything was about to come undone.

She drifted with painfully slow movements to the copper sink, supporting herself on the rim with rigid arms. Her hair covered her face. For a long while, silence—broken finally by the sound of tears plinking into the metal basin.

I grasped her arm and rubbed her back. "Hey," I said. "It's okay. It's all right."

"He's really gone," she rasped.

"You should clean up," I said.

She nodded shakily and turned on the faucet, splashing water on her face and working it over her hands and forearms, rinsing away most of the blood. Then she backed away from the sink, running her fingers down the collar of her blouse. Her hands trembled as she undid the thin, pearly buttons.

"Let me help," I said. Her arms fell to her sides, limp.

My fingertips grazed the soft skin of her sternum as I undid each button. Our foreheads were almost touching. When I finished the last one, she shrugged out of the stained blouse and let it drop to the floor.

A nearly imperceptible shiver flitted up my spine, and then fiery hands formed against the inside of my chest, pushing up and out.

Almost unconsciously, my hand moved to her waist. Her skin was warm. She made no move toward or away from me. My hand drifted down her leg and back up again, under her skirt, brushing against her thigh. I looked at her questioningly. For the first time in my life, I could not read her eyes.

"What about John?" she whispered.

I thought about my husband, all the way up in D.C., who kissed me every morning and held me at night, like he really meant it. From whom I stole things I didn't want and didn't need.

And I said, "He's dead."

Two words and we were caught in a fragment of a moment, that instant of suspended flight before a bird falls to earth, bullet in its breast.

The beginnings of a shocked apology formed on her lips, and I stopped it with my hands in her hair and my mouth on hers. The stiffness fled her body and it was like embracing a bundle of silk, her sliding against me, spilling through my arms and fingers. She melted in my grasp and I followed her to the floor, the edges of cold tile digging into my knees, something I'd long desired just out of reach.

THERE WAS ONE night, junior year of college, when Alexandra and I were sitting together on the floor of our dorm room. She'd been dating Graham for three months, and I'd already made up my mind about him. Those days, her face was rarely unguarded, but for a singular, precious moment, I saw her mask slip.

"Graham pushed me yesterday," she said without warning.

I made no attempt to hide my animosity. "What?"

Her shields immediately went back up, and I regretted speaking. "It was just a little tiff, that's all," she said. "I'm sorry. I shouldn't have brought it up."

"No," I said, "that's crazy. He has no right—"

"Anna," she said. "It's *nothing.*"

That night, I dreamt about her and Graham in bed. She was face up and he loomed over her. He had her by the shoulders and he was shoving her over and over into the bed, until she fell through the sheets and the mattress and the floor itself, disappearing from view.

THE FACILITY HAD rental cars so you could leave while they cleaned yours. And so I was driving home in a car that was not mine. Winter was approaching, and it was already getting dark. I gripped the wheel with both hands, so hard the tendons in my wrists began to hurt.

We had gotten up from the floor. She took my hand and held it, softly. Looked into my eyes. Something rippled across her face that I couldn't identify.

"I love Graham," she said. It was an apology.

I pulled my hand back, surprised at how quickly the warmth of her touch faded from my skin. I lowered my eyes and stepped away from her.

"You can clean up now," I said.

I redressed and stepped into the hallway, then waited until I heard her turn on the shower. I pressed my ear against the door and listened to the water wash me away.

How could I do this to myself? How could I be so stupid? Like a single moment of reprieve on the floor of a gilded bathroom changed anything at all.

My hands were burning now. I beat the steering wheel with the base of my palm, then again. My mouth tasted of salt. I missed the exit to my house, but I didn't care. I just kept driving. I drove without stopping, and soon it was completely dark and I was closer to Oklahoma than I was to Dallas.

John would be back soon. Maybe he already was. I could just disappear, drive away and never return. It started to storm. The taste of salt in my mouth.

Then there was a twinge in my chest, like something snapping under pressure. Paralyzing fingers full of crackling electricity radiated out from it, like nothing I'd ever felt before. My breath quickened, snagging on thorns that lined my throat. Don't fight it. Don't fight it. That's what they always said. It just makes it worse. My vision blurred. I jerked over to the shoulder of the road and saw my skin twisting, pulling, melting off my fingers down my arms and legs. I screamed and cried out, called Alexandra's name, but my lungs were on the outside of me, useless sacs against exposed ribcage, the comforting press of a diaphragm torn away. The steering wheel was slick with blood. *My* blood. Seeping into the mat beneath my feet. Smeared on the window, a blueprint of my undoing. The metallic tang crawled up and down my throat. Now my skull was splitting open. Now my heart was exploding in my chest.

And then. And then.

And then . . . I could still see my hands, trembling inches from my face, skin intact. My eyes refocused, and the car was free of blood. Heaving breaths, in and out. In and out. Hand against the base of my neck. Let it dissolve. Visions of quietus faded behind my eyes, and I was left shaking and alone on the side of the road, salt in my mouth, cars passing me by, the sound of thunder and night and *her* voice raging in my head a million miles away.

PHOEBE MURPHY is a writer of dark and speculative fiction. Her work also appears in *Nocturne Magazine*. She lives in Houston, Texas and will be pursuing an MFA in fiction at Texas State University. Visit her on Instagram @antinootus.

RAT SUIT KING

Patrick Barb

Derrick took his lunch break in Bryant Park, eating a bodega ham sandwich on a bench he shared with an old-school businessman who wore a crisp gray suit and a disapproving perma-glare. The man in the gray suit pulled his legs close together, striving for as much separation from Derrick as possible.

While Derrick was also dressed for work and he was also dressed in gray, the similarities ended there. On Derrick, the pajama-soft shag of the lower half of his mascot costume bulged over his black tennis shoes. The costumers sewed extra padding around the crotch of the outfit's lower half, which connected to similar padding placed inside the suit's upper portion. A long, pink tail sewed from felt scraps extended like some Muppet's penis from Derrick's padded backside, then dangled between the bench slats.

Upon further consideration, Derrick understood the true source of the businessman's disgust likely came from the cloth and foam rat's head, gray-furred with red mesh eyes, a black nose, and a yellow-toothed "smile" which had covered his face until he brought his take-out back to the bench. It was an ugly visage, all angular and gnarled. Derrick ran a nervous hand over his head, freeing sweat-plastered hair from where it had almost cemented itself to the top of his skull. The businessman wrinkled his nose and swung his legs around so he sat at an uncomfortable diagonal, nibbling at a rye bread sandwich with nervous squirrel-like energy.

Perhaps Mr. Businessman smelled Derrick's sweat and morning breath wafting from inside his rat mask. The younger man reached down, his hand wriggling to find purchase in the space between the musky interior of his costume bottoms and the slick, sweat-soaked gym shorts he wore after learning about the prevalence of fungal infections among his fellow street mascots. "Costume crotch," they called it, and one experience with it was more than enough for Derrick. His fingers closed around a tin of Altoids, which he worked up into the light like he'd become some claw machine made flesh.

Derrick smiled, relief whistling between clenched teeth once the tin emerged from his sweaty depths. He popped it open and downed three tablets. The mints carried a slight chemical odor, but he chalked it up to their less than sanitary storage conditions. His mouth pursed as the mints did their work. He moved to make eye contact with the businessman, hoping to exchange a look saying, *Is this better?*

But the businessman was gone, rushing away to finish his lunch elsewhere. He strode down the winding sidewalk, eyes forward and shoulders sharp.

And rushing in the opposite direction, *toward* Derrick, another man approached, wearing an expression also conveying immense displeasure with the lunching man in the rat costume. Derrick groaned, knew that no amount of Altoids would solve this fast-approaching problem.

"Hey, you! Hey, Derrick!"

The old man wasn't a dwarf, but close enough. He looked as though he'd be inconvenienced by a shrubbery at least. His skin was wrinkled, like laundry taken fresh from the washer and draped over the man's bones without a trip to the dryer first.

The top of the small man's head was crowned with shoe-polish black hair (and its odor up close made Derrick more than a little suspicious Chen used *actual* shoe polish for dying purposes). He wore a sleeveless undershirt and khaki pants held up with brown leather suspenders. He kept up his reprimanding chorus. "Derrick! Hey, boy, I'm talkin' to you!"

Spittle flew from the angry man's mouth as he came closer. With the precious time he knew was left, Derrick shoveled in a few more bites of salad, swallowing a hefty chunk of Crouton, before grabbing the mask and placing it over his head. "I know, Mr. Chen, I know!" He held his hands up, palms out. Tiny and pink inside the voluminous sleeves of his rat suit.

The Crouton and salad dressing went down the wrong tube. Derrick coughed, a wet, breadcrumb-caked sound fading into a belch. "Shit," he muttered, coming to grips with the fact he'd be stuck with the scent of stale salad burps swirling around his face for the rest of his shift.

Which happened to be the rest of the day.

As it turned out, off-the-books, mascot-costumed panhandlers didn't get eight-hour days or even lunch hours. They got whatever the hell Mr. Chen wanted to give them. Especially if they wanted enough of a cut to barely afford rent and keep the lights on. (And sometimes Derrick had to deal without having lights on or washing his clothes in Starbucks bathroom sinks.)

"What's rule number one?" Mr. Chen asked, arms folded across a sunken chest devouring the cloth of his T-shirt.

"Make people happy?" Derrick knew it wasn't the answer Chen sought, but he couldn't resist having fun with the man, his "boss," "handler," "pimp," or whatever he wanted to be called.

Chen took the bait. "No! No! No!" He shook his head and made X's with his arms to indicate just *how* wrong he believed Derrick was.

"You dressed like a rat. No one likes rats in New York City. People see rats, they say 'Ewww! Rat! Go away, rat!' They see *you,* they think the same thing. Except rat, a real rat, will just run away. Squeak-squeak, have a nice day. But you—you ask for money so you go away."

When he finished, Chen cocked an eyebrow toward Derrick, as if to say *Have I made myself clear?*

Derrick nodded. He was grateful that Chen did not notice his eyes rolling inside the costume head.

The older man picked up his admonishments where he'd left off. "Rule number one for always and forever: keep your costume on. No one sees you. No one knows you. They see rat. Only *rat.*"

Derrick stood, the round shadow of his inflated costumed body and the shabby circles of his ears, covering Mr. Chen in a black embrace. Every movement Derrick made felt exaggerated, the consequence of moving the bulky fabric around his lean and lanky body. "I'm sorry, Mr. Chen. I really am."

Mr. Chen shook his head once more, but this time lowered his arms from his chest. Despite the yelling and exploitative hours he inflicted on his employees, Derrick genuinely liked the man. After all, Chen took a chance on him when he believed the city was set to chew him up and spit him out. After the acting gigs he'd come to town expecting to land post-college never materialized—and even temping gigs dried up and withered away before he got enough time for the office administrators to remember his name—Derrick found himself teetering on the edge of becoming a cautionary tale.

"Hey! Hey! Hey! Quit dreaming. Okay?" Chen snapped his finger by the enlarged rat ears of Derrick's costume.

Derrick looked at his boss, the pink rat nose tilting upward until it nearly struck Chen's chin. The old man leaped back, surprisingly spry for his age—which fell somewhere between Derrick's dad's age and ancient, as far as the costume-wearer could tell. "Watch out," Chen muttered like he had avoided a leper's touch or some worse fate.

Derrick dropped to his knees, ready to focus and get back to work. The clear plastic bucket with "TIPS" written in Sharpie waited for him, with a pile of dirty bills and some tourists' pity spare change representing all of Derrick's earnings for the day. On the ground, with his rat-tail decorated ass poking out from under the bench, he felt more ridiculous than ever. But as he pulled the bucket closer, the sight waiting for him proved more shocking than anything he'd witnessed in the few years he'd spent in NYC.

Peeking out from under the abandoned grease-stained cellophane that once held another dime-a-dozen "authentic" New York pizza slice, an *actual* New York City sewer rat's tail swished and swiped across cracked cement and leaf particles. The wormy appendage with its gnawed-on pink flesh grazed Derrick's knuckle. Quick as possible, he drew his hand back to the gray fur of his costume, exhaling with a feverish hiss. Like a violently deflated beach ball. At the same time, instinct kicked in and he raised his head for a quick exit.

Too bad he hadn't moved far enough away for the necessary clearance. The top of his head struck a copper screw, oxidized green by weather and time. He moved so fast he felt the cold metal splitting through the fabric on the foam rat head, driven down to break the skin at the top of his actual head.

The warm trickle of blood from his scalp followed.

But before he registered the injury, Derrick's other senses were preoccupied with what happened before his eyes. Because when the stained mozzarella-encrusted cellophane fell away, Derrick found himself confronted by not one large black-furred, pink-faced rat with yellowed teeth hardened by time in the garbage cans and subway tunnels of Manhattan and the other boroughs, but a swarming storm cloud of the befouled rodents, four, five, ten, twenty. More. The hideous creatures writhed as one, undulating under splattered grease, making it impossible for Derrick to get an accurate count.

He watched the rats, tangled by their tails, through the black mesh eyes of his mask. He ignored the wet sensation at the back of his blood-slicked head until the wooziness threatened to overtake him. Their shit-stained tails interlocked into an elaborate knot-tying puzzle. Like if he reached in and grabbed the right tail he'd pull them all apart. He studied the vermin, hypnotized by their synchronized motion. Rather than crawl straight ahead or back and pull the mass in multiple directions at once, the rolling blob of rat flesh moved in a circle, rotating as one unit—like the Earth around the sun.

Until a triptych of rat heads stopped near Derrick's other hand, the one he'd left on the ground for balance when he'd pulled its partner close to him for safety. Like some murine Cerberus, the black-eyed rats opened their mouths and sunk teeth into the flesh of his exposed fingers. He pulled his entire body back, eyes watering so many actual tears. The scent of saltwater musk filled the costume.

"Motherfuck! Jesus!"

Mr. Chen's arms crossed again when Derrick straightened, wincing. Chen tapped his foot against the cement, as if to say *Well, time's wasting...*

Derrick pointed to the horde of rats hiding underneath the bench. Not considering how strange he must've appeared—a grown man in a rat costume used for panhandling, gesturing with violent fervor at the muck-encrusted rodent circle that attacked him.

"Rats! Rats! They're all stuck together, like a . . . like a . . ."

Except he lacked the words for what he'd witnessed.

"Yeah, yeah, okay, okay. Whatever you gotta do to get in character, boy," Mr. Chen said, waving a hand and dismissing the urgency Derrick tried to convey.

No one else in their vicinity moved in response or even acted like they noticed, beside a few hipsters and teens playing hooky, snapping pictures of the odd rat man. Their pictures might end up trending on social media for a few hours at best, then disappear, leaving nothing but a memory. Internet ephemera.

A low throbbing pain spread up Derrick's arm. He'd freed himself of the rats, but they'd done a number on him all the same. One took the skin off his fingertip, the other ground the wrinkled skin from a knuckle, and the third serrated the cuticle around a fingernail.

Thinking of the immediate pain and his desire to make someone understand, Derrick reached for Mr. Chen and pulled him to the bench. "Look!"

With his bloodied hand, he'd grabbed the old man by his suspenders. He pointed with a clean hand. But when Derrick peered through the slats, all he saw was the greasy cellophane pressed flat to the ground.

Then Mr. Chen's hand rested on the chest of his rat suit, pushing Derrick back with intense power. "Hey! You're bleeding, you know?"

Fat drops of scarlet fell from the scrapes, scratches, and bite marks on Derrick's hand. Some of the blood splattered on the ground. Some of it hit the bench. Some landed on Mr. Chen's bare mummified shoulders. And some got smeared across the grey fur of Derrick's rat costume.

To Derrick's surprise, Mr. Chen's next words weren't a reprimand. Even though his sharp expression suggested a man with retribution on his mind, he instead pointed to Derrick's wounded hand and said, "You need to go to a hospital, okay?"

Derrick shook his head, moving his rat snout back and forth. He didn't have the money for a trip to the emergency room or the patience for a free clinic. Plus, he figured he'd need as much money from his rat suit panhandling as he could manage.

Not that any of it was reaching him anytime soon. He wondered how much it'd cost to get his rat costume back to a state Mr. Chen would find acceptable.

"I'm fine," he said, before puking inside the rat head.

Mr. Chen put his hand over his eyes and turned away, leaving his employee to the remnants of his lunch dribbling into the body portion of his costume. "You owe me either a clean costume or a new costume. Okay?"

Okay.

"FOUR HUNDRED FUCKING dollars!" Derrick's voice cracked as he bemoaned the cost of a replacement costume, alone in his apartment. Everything he'd found online from Amazon to eBay suggested a three-figure investment was required if he hoped to attain a replica of the costume used by Mr. Chen in his menagerie of panhandling larger-than-life characters.

Of the costumed panhandlers he stationed across the city, Chen worked with children's TV show monsters, superheroes, and a bunny—who was or wasn't an Easter Bunny depending on the time of the year. Derrick was his only rat. As a result, he wore Mr. Chen's only rat costume.

Sitting at the found-on-a-street-corner table in his kitchen, Derrick upturned the stained costume's head to take another look at the musty interior. The insides stank of Lysol from the bathroom and some potpourri shavings he'd stolen from an unmanned counter at Macy's. Derrick hoped the brown chunks would work like sawdust in elementary school classrooms whenever a kid hurled and the janitor didn't want to invest too much time or effort cleaning.

However, this time, Derrick played both kid and clean-up man. His fingers were marred by dried blood turned black and yellowed blisters he prayed weren't signs of infection. Mindful of the tenderness of his injuries, he brushed aside the matted fur poking through the inside of the mascot's head until he found the tag.

Rex Rattus: 1 of ?

Derrick pulled his hand back like he'd touched a livewire. He brought his injured fingers to chapped lips.

He had no clue what *Rex Rattus: 1 of ?* meant. He didn't know if it referred to a company or a costume type or what.

Frustration taking a firm hold, Derrick banged his other hand against the tabletop, hitting the birdshit-splattered wood so hard his broke-down laptop launched upward and then landed on its side. The next thing he knew, some warm and wet substance dribbled down his chin.

Only then, he realized he'd nibbled open the wounds on his hand, and bled anew onto his costume. Making it much harder to clean.

"Awww shit."

Though it wasn't like any cleaner he'd tried, via phone calls or in-store appearances, it showed a willingness to accept the assignment. The in-person visits resulted in wrinkled noses, evil eye stares, and one zealous Hispanic woman repeating a litany of *Ave Marias,* while pushing Derrick out the door of her shop. Phone calls weren't much better, though they lacked the added sting of having someone else witness embarrassment reddening his gaunt cheeks.

As a result, buying a replacement suit—despite Derrick having nowhere close to the necessary funds—presented itself as the most viable of the impossible options.

In other words, he was well and truly screwed.

NOT TO MENTION the pounding headache Derrick endured all day, kicked off by a rude awakening from his roommates as they rose, showered, and departed for their 9 to 5's, making thinking hard in general.

It wasn't that his roommates were loud or obnoxious. Far from it. Derrick trended more toward black sheep, while Keith, Lamont, and Trix were all nose-to-the-grindstone, keep-your-head-down-and-do-the-work kind of New Yorkers. With their publishing, tech start-up, and finance jobs, the trio existed as the epitome of the dream Derrick brought to the big city. They had managed not to stumble out of the starting gate, though.

The morning after Derrick saw the tangle of rats and stained his costume, his roommates' normally subdued routines sounded like a subway train screeching to a halt on silver tracks, sparks striking old bricks and cement, exploding his dreams into a million fragments. He hid under the stiff underwashed covers on his cot (the one bed that fit in the converted closet space serving as his bedroom), awaiting their departure.

The back of his head aching, he exited the room nose first, sniffling. Staring at his bedraggled reflection in the gunmetal-grey surface of the fridge, Derrick discovered he'd kept the rat costume on all evening. When he took the mask off, his hair sat plastered on his head, stuck in place by sweat and dried sick. He felt certain he'd reached his lowest point. Not just since moving to New York. But of all time.

DERRICK'S EYES GLAZED over as he reviewed his Craigslist post:

"Seeking **SPECIAL** *Mascot Costume: Rattus Rex?"*

He'd managed to upload some photos of the rat costume, propped up against the far wall of his bedroom. Lucky for him, he'd snuck a peek at a scrap of paper on his roommates' desk with the wi-fi password on it. (Apartment consensus at the time was that Derrick shouldn't have access until he switched to paying his share of the rent with cash and not IOUs.)

He listed his posting under special requests. The way Derrick saw it, someone would have to be *special*—as in the touched in the head variety—to own another costume like the strange, creepy rat one Mr. Chen had loaned him.

Speaking of the devil, as soon as Derrick's finger pressed the Return key confirming he wanted to post the ad, his old cellphone, a blocky and cracked monstrosity, rattled against the tabletop.

Caller ID: CHEN.

Derrick leaned back in his rickety chair, considering the light emanating from the screen as though he'd recovered the Holy Grail. He pulled the phone close, pressing it tight to the side of his face. "Hello?"

"Hey, boy, you working today or what?"

"But I don't have . . . it's not my day. I worked . . . "

A long pause followed from the other end of the line as Derrick flailed, scrambling to bring up the calendar on his laptop. His heart dropped to his stomach as he read the date in his toolbar. Not just one day had passed since the rat costume debacle, but two. Remembering to exhale, his breath whistled through his teeth and into the phone line to Mr. Chen.

"Yeah, you're late. Got my costume cleaned yet, too?"

The words sounded clear as a bell in Derrick's head, so it made no sense when Chen cleared his throat and spoke the words again. "Yeah, you're late. Got my costume cleaned yet, too?"

"Yes, sir. I—you didn't give me a chance to answer."

"What the hell're you talking about, boy? I didn't say nothing to you until now."

Derrick found himself struck by the overwhelming urge to drop to the ground, imagining Mr. Chen standing in the back of some noisy market, on the phone with his wayward employee. In this vision, Chen stood in Derrick's path.

He pictured the raised cuffs of the old man's khakis lifted above the ankle, showing enough skin for Derrick to turn his head and take a bite. Teeth piercing flesh, saliva mingling with fast-pooling blood.

"You okay?"

Mr. Chen's query interrupted Derrick's reverie. A translucent sheen of drool decorated the young man's chin. He wanted to end the call. Needed to end the call. He intended to say something short, simple, and to the point. "I understand, sir. I'll be out soon. And as for the costume, I'm trying to find a replacement. Don't worry, I'll spare no expense."

But what came out of Derrick was a series of gut-rumbling grunts and high-pitched squeals. He hit "End Call" fast as possible. Threw the phone across the room where it bounced off the makeshift plywood door to his room.

As if it had a life of its own, the phone leaped into the opening where the rat costume head connected to the rat costume body. Swallowed by the darkness, the phone-screen's ambient light was absorbed and thinned by its new confinement.

Derrick leaned forward, fingers stretching to their limit. Before making contact, the sickly green phone-screen lit up. Buzzing vibrations shook the costume, causing the hollowed-out rat to shift, appearing ready to hop off the wall and crawl on its own. Derrick's hand closed around the phone and he pulled it back to his face.

Someone was calling, but he didn't recognize the number.

Before he answered, another call came in.

Then another. And another. On and on . . .

Derrick sat crosslegged on the laundry-strewn floor watching the calls come in. Sometimes a text message blipped across the screen. The initial trickle of communication morphed into a deluge of confirming messages. Derrick had been mistaken—plenty of people owned an extra rat suit.

When he worked up the nerve to check his messages, each stated the same thing: "I have *Rattus Rex,* 2 of ?," " . . . 3 of ?," " . . . 4 of ?"

One after the other, counting up with no end in sight. Derrick stopped counting when he got to "19 of ?" There wasn't much point in going further.

Strange enough that he'd placed his classified ad five minutes previous.

He also had to contend with the fact he hadn't included his phone number in the listing.

DERRICK STEPPED OUT from the subway entrance at Union Square, eyeing buskers and other non-costumed panhandlers. His rat suit still smelled terrible. He couldn't for the life of him remember why he'd opted to wear the stained and damaged costume instead of carrying it with him. Maybe in an oversized garbage bag—fitting luggage for the hideous outfit. Of course, he also wasn't sure why he'd brought it in the first place.

To compare it to the others, he told himself with a feigned confidence he hoped would quell his raging nerves—despite all evidence to the contrary.

At least his roommates would be happy with the suit gone. When he'd emerged from his room near the end of the day, they were waiting, standing outside the door in a semi-circle of judgment with their heads bowed. Derrick stood with the rat's head tucked under his arm. Not to be intimidated by the prejudices of his roommates, he walked the gauntlet, showing each the tag. "What's this mean?"

They were smart. Capable too. Certainly more than Derrick the failure. Keith and Lamont wrinkled their noses, sneering at Derrick as though he'd come up to them shit-faced drunk with puke all over the front of his shirt. (Which wasn't too far from the truth.) Trix appeared set to react the same, but they stopped themselves. They read the tag with an eyebrow raised. "Rattus Rex?" they asked.

Derrick nodded, as the matted fur of the costume's neckline tickled the space between his chin and Adam's apple.

"It's Latin. Means *Rat King.*"

With that said, Trix lowered their eyes and ducked away from the semi-circle of judgment, miming like they were busy with some minor dishes-related matter in the kitchen.

Derrick returned silence in kind, hoping his uncertainty showed through. Trix coughed, breaking the thick, roiling tension between the roommates. Then, they said, "You know like when a bunch of rats get their tails all tangled. It's an urban legend though. People say they become like one many-headed creature. Working as one. Total bullshit, though."

I saw one.

When no one answered, Derrick tried again.

I SAW ONE.

His roommates locked eyes with him, their lips closed, but Derrick heard them inside his head. Speaking as one.

Please leave.

So, he did. Because he wanted to prove them wrong. He wanted to prove *everyone* wrong. His parents. His teachers. The acting coaches who'd overpromised and underdelivered. His roommates. Mr. Chen.

Derrick hadn't told Mr. Chen to come, but he showed up regardless. His shirt was still stained from Derrick's two-day-old vomit. The sight made the young man wonder how badly Chen needed the percentage he took from all his panhandlers.

As the sun set behind the massive towering buildings of Manhattan, blacking out swaths of cement and asphalt, the old man tottered forward on unsteady legs. Limping as though his ankle were bitten, like Derrick daydreamed.

"Shit." Derrick hoped he'd remembered in time, hoped he'd sighted his elderly boss before the old man caught him. He pulled the rat's head over his face, inhaling caked-in puke, sweat, and the salt of his tears. But at least he wore the right visage for the job. At least he wouldn't get yelled at.

He waved his tiny pink hands. Staring across the gap between them on the brick walkway, he hoped Chen would approve. But when the old man caught sight of his wayward employee, Derrick looked past him. In the span of seconds, something else caught the young man's eye.

Viewed through the black of the rat head, Derrick caught another person wearing a Rattus Rex costume, waving *their* tiny pink hands. They emerged from behind a bush or a tree, it was hard to say. One moment, Mr. Chen limped forward, cheeks sucking in and out with each labored breath and pained step, then another rat appeared.

Derrick lowered his hand. He positioned it near the neck of his costume, prepared to discard the bulky headpiece once more. After all, shouldn't he want to meet the costume-seller face to face? Human face to human face. But he stopped himself. A voice spoke in his head. *"Don't."*

It was his voice, the inner monologue playing inside his head at all times. Same as anyone else might experience. But it was *more.* Like there was an echo in his skull, bouncing off the insides. A distant chorus, as though marchers were heading down Fifth Avenue to the Park. Almost chanting his inner monologue in harmony.

Almost.

When Mr. Chen moved close enough to take in Derrick and his soiled rat costume, he stopped short. Derrick watched the interloping rat coming up behind his boss. He expected the stranger not to stop in time. He'd pictured the rat costume's bulky mid-section colliding with the old man.

But the second rat proved nimbler than expected, coming to a halt short of contact. A heavy wind blew between the concrete and steel buildings surrounding the Park, then dipped lower to wriggle through the surrounding trees.

As a result, Derrick couldn't hear much over the whistling and shrieks. He settled for trying to lip-read Chen's trembling mouth and follow the pantomime hand and head gestures of the other rat. It appeared as though this second rat spoke first. In response, Mr. Chen turned his head, eyes widening when he came face to snout with this other costume-wearer. When he returned to gaze at Derrick, waiting for both his boss and the rat-man to walk closer, Chen appeared confused, like he'd been hit on the head.

Derrick looked lower and saw the man's too-thick socks stuffed into his shoes, already turning salmon.

I should do something. I should say something.

Derrick stepped forward, moving to join the fear-frozen Mr. Chen and this new rat. But when he took his first step, the impact sent psychic ripples through concrete and brick, passing over Chen and linking Derrick to his new rat companion. He saw an Asian man, not as young as Derrick, not as old as

Chen. A narrow-cheeked, quiet, unassuming figure, compelled by some force he couldn't explain to leave a promising career in the government back in the home country to travel a dangerous path to America. Finding himself unwanted by all. Not looking for a fight, but always ending up in one. Black eyes and blood-crusted nostrils. The need to feel something, to connect in some way. But afraid to show his bruised and battered face.

Then, he found the rat costume. When he wore it, the other man never asked for anything. He didn't want donations of money or food or booze, no offers of shelter either. He'd refuse them all with a curt shake of his rat's head. He wanted to wear the costume and be near people. That's all he wanted.

At the same time, as Derrick experienced all of this, the young man felt his life, his story traveling out to the other man. An exchange of ideas, states of being.

"Derrick?"

Mr. Chen's question came as an afterthought, barely noticed between the two men in their costumes.

"More?"

This time, the pair of men in rat costumes heeded the old man's query. As Derrick stood opposite his counterpart, they turned their foam- and felt-covered heads, watching more costume-wearers emerge. Some wore the costume loose, others cinched it so tight one could make out the outlines of belly buttons and beer guts. When the others came close enough, Derrick stumbled on the cracked concrete.

A flood of faces and stories washed over him.

An African American kid from the Marcy Projects, trading

in candy bars and subway dance shows for the Rattus Rex.

A college student from Bard, her hair in dreadlocks and skin the color of the year's first snowfall. Black eye-liner, black lips, a choker. She wore the costume for her clients.

Some faces, like Derrick's, were variations on a theme.

They formed a circle around Mr. Chen. His stained shoes and sweat-soaked sleeveless tee were close to glowing amid the sea of grey fur. His mumbling, panicked breath provided the backing track.

Inside his head, Derrick enjoyed twenty, thirty, fifty conversations all at once. Each one understood and clear.

Something scraped against the back of a nearby bench. Derrick's head turned and his rat face moved with him. Whiskers again scraped other whiskers.

The last arrival emerged. Derrick beamed.

The businessman, the one who'd turned away in disgust that afternoon when Derrick first glimpsed the rat king.

Except maybe it wasn't disgust showing on the man's face. Maybe those lines etched on his brow and around his harsh, thin lips came from jealousy.

Regardless of past intention, Derrick waved the man closer.

The circle was complete.

Mr. Chen was on the ground, pushing against grey-covered legs, trying to carve a path out. He wouldn't succeed.

Working as one already, the assembled rat costume wearers turned their backs to each other. Their faces were all the same on the outside after all. So what did it matter if they saw each other? Derrick shuddered, and the low moans and gasping squeaks of his fellow rats told him others were experiencing something similar. The long pink tail that hung loose behind bench slats slithered and writhed against his backside.

It stiffened, poking out straight, again reminding Derrick of some abominable erection. Then it sprung out, pulling him backward. The tail of the costume wearer behind him did the same until the two met in the middle.

Wrapped around and around and around each other. Then another tail came from a diagonal. And another from the side. Another and another. When they connected, the faces Derrick observed faded from his memory. As though they were becoming a part of him.

One after the other. Connecting to Derrick and giving themselves away. Until the last tail, that of the businessman, all clean and pristine, probably straight out of a new costume bag and sent to the man at God only knew what cost.

When they linked and the man's face faded from memory, Derrick flexed. Ripples sent out like shockwaves, moved the other costume-wearers. Those nameless, faceless, story-less parts of the Rat Suit King.

Through the mesh-eyes of his suit, as well as all the others, Derrick observed the world. It was New York City after all. The world in microcosm. A world long ago given to the rats even if the humans stuck around, persistent in not getting the message.

Derrick's eyes bled a creamy red, like tomato sauce, leaking through the mesh of the rats' eyes. Soon, there was no Derrick. No distinction between that being's head and the others.

There was only the Rat Suit King.

THE RAT SUIT King found the old man crawling across the waste of a knocked over garbage can. Moving in a pinwheel pattern, arms outstretched and yellow teeth gnawing through the fabric, the Rat Suit King fell upon the man like a buzzsaw. Biting, gnashing, clawing. Consuming flesh and drinking blood, its whiskers awash in gore. Scraps of clothing and broken bones secreted away for building its nest.

When the feast was complete, the Rat Suit King and all its bodies, tails, and heads fled into the shadows. As filling as the old man was, a morsel pulled apart and savored, the Rat Suit King needed the darkness to lick its wounds, to let gangrenous rot set in, to let its legend grow.

All across the park, faces bobbing like drunken fireflies. Someone bearing witness to a transformation. Ten, twenty, fifty visages becoming one. A murmured chorus set to spread across the boroughs.

All hail the Rat Suit King!

All hail!

PATRICK BARB is an author of weird, dark, and horrifying tales, currently living (and trying not to freeze to death) in St. Paul, Minnesota. His works include the dark fiction collection *Pre-Approved for Haunting,* the novellas *Gargantuana's Ghost* and *Turn,* as well as the novelette *Helicopter Parenting in the Age of Drone Warfare.* His forthcoming works include the themed short-story collection *The Children's Horror* from Northern Republic Press and the sci-fi/horror novel *Abducted* from Dark Matter Ink. His 2023 short story "The Scare Groom" was selected for *Best Horror of the Year Volume 16.* Visit him at patrickbarb.com.

TAKE THIS BODY

M.C. St. John

"The problem with this village," Kellen Turner, the sin eater, said, "is that no one tries to be better."

From his deathbed—a hay sack suspended by a thin web of ropes—Turner shifted to take in those who surrounded him. They were faces he knew well, faces hovering in the shadows of his hut, cast in the guttering light of candles from his dining table.

The first to speak was Henry McClellan, the mayor, who was always the first to raise his voice on public matters. He puffed up his chest, gave a great theatrical sigh, and tilted his head just so, allowing his concerned eyes to glisten by the candlelight for all to see.

"I hardly think that is fair to say. Our village has prospered over the years, and to whom do we owe the auspice? Why, the strong backs of farmers, the dusty hands of bakers' wives, the keen eye of carpenters. It is by no accident we have reaped our bounty. Everyone has had their part to play."

Turner laughed. It sounded like a scullery maid scraping a rusty pot. "Spoken like a true politician, crowd-pleasing with no substance. Your father, if he were still alive, would be proud of such a speech. Mayor begetting mayor from one generation to the next." He leered with sunken eyes. "Pretty words cover all matters of sin, do they not?"

McClellan smoothed his waistcoat. The gold chain of his pocket watch trembled. "I don't know what you're getting at."

"Come now. The high taxes in this village are nothing new. They are the very ones your father had devised. The added coin afforded the village grain mill, yes, but it also paid for Conrad's silk shirts and cravats and concubines . . . "

"Lies. *Mendacity.*"

" . . . and yet you stand here at my bedside, fussing and fidgeting. Frightened of losing what your father so readily had of my services, when he required them at his end . . . "

When Turner attempted to laugh again, he choked on something wet and thick. He retched, his gnarled fist pressed to his mouth. The thin ropes of his bed threatened to snap.

Stephen Ames, the village doctor, stepped in to help. He placed one hand on Turner's shoulder to steady the old man; Ames placed the other hand on the man's brow. "He's burning like a stoked forge," he said, and gestured to a young woman holding a black leather bag. "Alice, fetch me the jar of leeches to draw out the poison—"

"*No.*"

Turner convulsed, wracked with his coughing fit. After a time, he wheezed and caught the blockage, screwed shut his eyes, and swallowed. But after the effort, Turner did not fall back into his bed. He instead shot up halfway and latched onto the back of Ames's neck. His rasping breath filled the silence.

"You know full well no creature can remove what's inside me," he said. "No creature save one."

"We can try again." Ames blinked before Turner's unflinching gaze. "M-modern medicine can help you, and can h-help this village, all of us."

"There is only one way. My own."

Then Turner sniffed, his nostrils flaring. He inhaled deeply and shivered.

"It's incredible," he said, "that given my sorry state I am still hungry. I smell the lust inside you, like freshly roasted lamb chops. It is not lamb, of course. What is sin if not deception? But I yearn for it—*always.*"

His fevered gaze settled on Alice, the nursemaid. Turner grinned.

"Doctor," he said, "what would your wife Susan say about *your* hungers?"

With a disgusted cry, Ames wriggled out of Turner's grip. The doctor opened his mouth to say something to Alice, but the nursemaid lowered her eyes, gripped the black leather bag, and said nothing. Murmurs from others ran through the hut.

"My Lord," McClellan said.

Ames glared. "You're one to judge. Turner himself said it of your coffers. You wax poetic about the bounties of our village as you rob the laborers blind. Greed, pure and simple. But no one here believes the money goes only to paying for your fancy clothes. Is flesh not another of your vices, Henry? Like father, like son?"

"How can *you* perpetuate such hearsay? 'He who is without sin cast the first stone.' Father Gray from his pulpit taught us that simple warning as children."

McClellan again ran his hands down his waistcoat. But no matter how many times he tried, he failed to smooth out the wrinkles. Frustrated, he threw a petulant glance at the figure closest to the dining table. "Father Gray, *tell them.*"

Rodderick Gray, the priest, stirred from the shadows. Unlike the others, however, he kept his distance from Turner's bedside. He clutched a Bible against his vestments.

"Indeed, we are all with sin," he said, "and to judge another man without first looking into one's own heart for such faults is hypocrisy in the eyes of the Lord."

Father Gray frowned. He forced his eyes upon the creature slouched in its bed. "Did I say something amusing?"

Turner attempted to hide his grin, failed, and waved his crooked hands in surrender. "Where do I start, Father? Perhaps let's start with . . . all of it."

"You *question* scripture? Someone of your *lowly* station?"

"I question the person who espouses the word of God and ignores the truth before his eyes." And here, Turner's face grew stony. "The church does not acknowledge me or my role. Yet

I am the one in this village who does the work you claim to do every Sunday."

"Confession absolves us of our sins," Father Gray said. "As do the last rites given to those who are ready to pass from this world into heaven. It is the Lord's work alone that can accomplish these hallowed tasks."

Turner again sniffed the air. "I recognize that stench of aged cheese anywhere." He smacked his lips and nodded. "*Pride.*"

"This man is an abomination," Father Gray said. "There is no cleansing him. He is riddled with sin . . . in mind, body, and soul."

"Is that what you were planning to do? *Save* me?"

Turner stared at the wavering faces. Only the sizzling of the candle wicks answered him, the wax pooling down to puddles on the table. Soon the fire would be gone.

"There is no saving *me,*" he said. "There's only saving yourselves now."

He pointed a bony finger at each of them.

"You all speak of your importance in the village. Let me remind you of my duty, the one I have served long before Father Gray had come to roost in his parish. *I am a sin eater.* You may cast your eyes away as I walk down the village road in my rags and bare feet. But when one of your kith or kin died unexpectedly, before Father Gray could serve last rites? Why, you were the first to knock on my door with the promise of food."

Ruffled, Father Gray thumped his Bible against his chest. "We need not hear any more of this charlatan's tongue—"

"But you do."

The timbre of Turner's voice was the crackle of firewood

in a hearth, the rush of embers in the flue of his dark throat.

Father Gray was silenced.

"You must hear," Turner said, "because you all have been part of *my* congregation. You know my rituals. In the dead of night, you all have taken me to a house with a cooling body. You all have lain a loaf of bread upon the breast of the corpse, as instructed. You all know that the bread serves my purpose, that it is a vessel to sop up leftover sins."

Now Turner's eyes grew black, the pupils expanding, eating up the irises.

"Father Gray has lied to you. Sin is not absolved. It never goes away. It may leave one body, but it lingers . . . unless eaten by another." Turner tapped his own chest. "*I* took the bread, sodden with vice. I chewed and savored the various ills. Lust, pride, greed, and the others, yes, but other, more exotic transgressions too. Murder, fornication, torture—ah, the feasts I have had from the dead of this village . . . "

A sudden thump on the dirt floor startled the others. They stared at Alice. From her pale, shaking hands she had dropped the doctor's bag. Her chest heaved, her throat clicked, her pallid cheeks puffed in and out. She spun away, gagging.

"Yes," Turner said, "it raises the gorge, doesn't it? It did for me at first. But the taste becomes intoxicating. I craved it. And when villagers saw what evils it drew from their lost loved ones? The true, *ugly* sins? The next logical step was for the villagers to rid themselves of sin while they were still alive."

Ames went to comfort Alice. He glowered at Turner. "You are disgusting *and* mad."

"Am I now? Tell me, doctor, have you figured out why I

am dying? You have not. No amount of modern medicine has answered the riddle, nor has it discredited the answer I know to be true. *I have overeaten my fill.*"

Then Turner's own throat bobbed and trembled. The wet lump again filled his windpipe, stifling his breath. He wheezed and hacked harder than before, this time the wisps of gray hair fluttering from his skull. The bed frame knocked against the dining table. A candle tilted over and fell to the floor. The flame, sputtering but alive, illuminated a patch of dirt.

McClellan's face blanched. "He is *choking*. S-somebody help him. Ames, can't you do something, one last time . . . ?"

Ames grabbed his black bag from the floor and tossed it before the mayor's well-polished shoes. "If you're so hellbent on saving him, why don't you do it? Get your hands dirty from actual work for once in your life."

McClellan made to say more, but Turner's retching grew more violent. The death rattle was upon the sin eater. His thin frame expanded like a bellows, shuddered, and threatened to collapse. His throat bulged, his Adam's apple darkening.

Finally, Turner pounded his chest once, twice . . . and something loosened in one great upchuck of exhalation.

A black glob, trailing bile and spit, flew from his mouth.

The surrounding villagers fell back. Slowly, they leaned in for a closer look. Their collective gaze landed on the dying candle and the wavering light it cast upon the ground.

The black glob glistened there, floating in a puddle of saliva. It looked like a rotten egg sitting in a skillet. The mass hissed and steamed as if it was cooking on a stove. The hut was suddenly filled with its hot stench. The others covered their noses and blinked away tears.

Father Gray smelled brimstone.

Ames smelled embalming chemicals.

Alice smelled rotten flowers.

McClellan smelled a whore's perfume.

And then the black mass writhed and began folding in on itself. As it shrunk, the stench intensified. The hiss rose to a noxious shriek. Then, in one acrid puff of smoke, the mass vanished. A burnt spot in the dirt floor was all that remained.

"Lord have mercy," Father Gray said, and crossed himself.

"I find that unlikely," McClellan said.

"It's gone," Ames said.

Alice stared at the ground. Her voice was tender, frightened. "But where did it go? Turner said the sin doesn't vanish."

"I'll tell you where," Turner said. "Into the earth."

Ames groaned. "Let me guess . . . to Hell?"

"I'm not as mystical as Father Gray. I don't believe in Hell. But I do know what's *very real* beneath our village. The aquifer." Turner's face was solemn. "Sin is working its way to the clean water. It will disperse and move with the current, come out of the ground in streams to the river. It will turn the mill wheel, feed the livestock, settle in the drinking wells. It will do what sin always does: seek hosts. What's the phrase, Father? Ah yes, *be fruitful and multiply*."

"And there's no way to stop it?" McClellan asked.

"The bit that got away? I'm afraid not."

"What about the rest of it?" Alice asked. Her eyes fell to Turner's stomach, which lay exposed above the unwashed bed linen. The stomach was grotesquely large on his emaciated frame. It rivaled the size of many pregnant women and ornery sows that Alice had assisted Doctor Ames in birthing. "What will happen when you—?"

"*That,* my dear, is what I've been trying to tell you all night," Turner said. "My ability is supposed to be used as a last resort, a safeguard for the village. *Be better, so you will not need me.* But nobody has heeded the warning. They have tempted me with their delicious sins, knowing all they need is bread to break with me and they will be cleansed. Like some people have in this very hut."

Rather than pause to allow the others to worry and wring their hands, Turner hurried on. His voice was growing raspy and faint. The fallen candle sputtered out. The hut darkened.

"I once was hungry and painfully alive. Now I am gorged and dying. Is that how God works? He and His mysterious ways? I do not know. All I know is the power of consequence. Even if you cared to bury me, it would be a terrible mistake. What I told you of that small sin escaping to the aquifer is true. Imagine if *all of me* reached into the water."

"The village would be doomed." McClellan jerked his hand down his waistcoat. His thumb caught the watch chain and broke it. "There would be no way to recover. Not without another of your kind."

"There is none," Father Gray said, staring at his Bible. "I made sure of it years ago."

"Pride before the fall," Turner said. Another coughing fit hit, and he fought back as much as he could to speak.

" . . . burning me on a pyre would be worse. Ash and sin swirling in the air, both smelling of char. No, there is no good way to dispose of a sin eater." Then the coughing turned dry and weak and curiously hollow.

"Except one," Ames said.

The doctor was pale as he left Alice and walked past McClellan. He stepped over the doctor's bag on the ground. Father Gray retreated from his position as Ames approached the dining table. Sitting upon the wood, flickering in fading candlelight, was a massive loaf of baked bread. Next to it was a crude knife.

Without a word, Ames took the knife and began cutting. The soft smell of wheat flour rose, briefly scented the air, and vanished.

By the time the doctor came to his bedside, Turner had sunk into his hay sack bed. The ropes vibrated with his hacking. His eyes were completely black but fixed on Ames. When Turner saw what the doctor was doing, the old man curled his lips into a smile. After one final cough, the sin eater died with that smile still on his face. It slowly stiffened to a sneer.

McClellan was the first to speak, as always.

"It can't be. What about the leeches, Ames? Like you said?"

But Ames shook his head. "*We* are the leeches. We were before. We must be now."

He placed four pieces of bread on Turner's stomach. A piece for each of them, the first of the townsfolk. The freshly baked bread immediately turned gray and soggy, and then blackened and swelled. Steam rose in curls, carrying its hot stench to each of them.

Below the pieces, Turner's stomach may have shrunk, or perhaps it was a trick of the firelight. There was certainly more bread to break tonight to find out. More sin to mete out, bit by bit. Father Gray could toll the church bell to awake the village. McClellan could convince the people of an emergency ceremony. The bakers' wives could be sent to bake more bread if needed. More bread for the bakers, the farmers, the carpenters, the rich men, the concubines, and all the rest. Everyone would be welcome tonight at the wake of Kellen Turner, the sin eater. It would take all of them to pay their respects.

Ames picked up the darkest piece. It was hot to the touch. Hot and *alive*. He held it up for all to see.

"Do this in remembrance of him," he said.

Then Ames cast a sad glance to Alice, closed his eyes long enough for a prayer, and took the body into his own.

M.C. St. JOHN is the author of the short story collection *Other Music*. His stories have appeared, as if by luck or magic, in *Cosmorama*, *Flame Tree Publishing*, *Tales of Sley House*, and *Thirteen Podcast*. He is also a member of the Great Lakes Association of Horror Writers, serving as co-editor for the horror anthology *Recurring Nightmares*. See what he's writing next at www.mcstjohn.com.

DR. BLACKWOOD'S MIDNIGHT GHOST SHOW

Mathew L. Reyes

We stumbled out of the bar just before midnight on that long-ago evening, a real bluster-dead sort of night. Exchanging the sweating bodies and technicolor lights for cool air and the no-sounds of a dilapidated city, we sighed, let our hearts calm. Around us towered skyscrapers, those derelict vestiges of man's avarice, which blocked the natural darkness of the sky. The shadows of these cyclopean things stretched over us, defying the glow of the street lights, tried to swallow us as we walked and jostled each other down the dirty sidewalks.

Strewn along the cracked cement was trash of all varieties, a delicacy of decay. Greasy wrappers mingled with rotted food and stale cigarette leavings. The smell of some vagrant's vomit drifted from steaming pavement.

"Breezers," one of my friends said, "who was that, shit the pavement?"

"Wasn't me," I said. I hugged my jacket close, as though it would protect me from the pressing stench and darkness closing around us. Every time we stepped out of the light of one streetlamp it felt as though we'd fall into an abyss or trip over something dead and abandoned, a thing unseen. Yet we passed into the next dome of light, and the next, until we neared the old theatre district.

The *Orpheum* on Hennepin Avenue was the only one left in operation. Its distant marquee lights were on, adding to the sense that we might still be in the living world and not some blasted afterlife where the darkness itself was the only blooded, breathing creature.

How quickly the sensation of life died after we left that sweltering club of lust, wandering hands, and blacklight teeth. How firmly was the idea of my own smallness implanted within me along these towering office ruins.

In those times it was our habit to wander the streets at night. There was nothing else to do. Dayside we worked. I had ten-hour shifts in one of the crumbling offices processing data acquisition forms. My pallies worked near the same. So nightside we wandered. Drinking and dancing, drinking more, then wandering without aim around the city. Drifting, more like.

There were four of us, and those seedy elements who raped, robbed, and murdered did not have the spine to approach groups. So we wandered empty streets, peering into dead shops and kicking cans and laughing at abandoned window displays. There would be holiday dioramas evoking some extinct era, the fashion and decor alien to us.

We did not laugh at all the shopfronts, though.

From some of the empty stores there leered, from the darkness, pale mannequins. Their hands would be stretched out to us, as though beckoning us to join them, to try on their dusty clothes, to wear their plastic skin. A few, having long ago fallen against the glass, looked as though they'd spent the last of their energy trying to escape—to get away *to* something or *from* something it was never clear, but I couldn't bear looking at them. Though they had no eyes, I felt their stare as we passed, and a creeping tightness scratched its way under my skin.

When we arrived at the *Orpheum,* its marquee declared that it was still running a performance of *Pagliacci.* A mannequin made up like the clown stood near the box office. Its white, silky costume fluttered in the fetid wind. The sun-bleached pompoms on his front wobbled to and fro. On some nights we'd see the play, revel as the clown murdered his wife and her lover on the stage. But the rivers of blood that soaked the oak floor on every performance had lost their magic, as had the dying screams and glint of the blade upon raw skin. The music still had its charm, but it wasn't enough.

One of my friends paused. "Anybody fancy the show?"

"Not tonight," another said. "Breezers, it's always the same one. Has been since—well, I don't know."

"Fairly sure," our fourth replied, "it's always been *Pagliacci.*"

"That can't be," I said. "And at any rate we've seen it enough. I've had my fill of bodies at the club, and my fill of blood at the late-night theatre show. I'm done with Pag-the-Clown."

For a moment, there was a bit of a tuffle, with two of us wanting to see the show again and the other two objecting. Our options were limited. We could go back to the club, reinsert ourselves into the sea of sweating bodies and lights; there was the show, true, but it had long lost its charms; wandering the streets until dawn, picking up fifths of gin and whiskey along the way, was another way to go, but my belly was done up with booze for the night.

As we bickered, the wind picked up, and something thin and wispy fluttered from the dark beyond the lights. It slapped my shins gently and came to a stop. A flyer.

I picked it up.

"Huh," I said.

"What's that?"

The paper was bright yellow, so incandescent and artificial that it hurt my eyes. I believe there was a crayon (when I was younger and the world was not so colored in with greys and browns) called "laser lemon" that had a violent effect on the eyes. It hurt to read the large, black letters, but I read it a few times before handing it around.

"A new show," I said.

One of my companions raised his eyebrow and pushed his dark hair from his face. "Could be real cattywumps like, could be." He handed it to the other two, who read it and then passed it back to me. I glanced again at the words, reading each carefully to ensure I'd not misread the remarkable and somewhat unsettling message:

<u>DOCTOR A.M. BLACKWOOD</u>

presents…

Midnight Ghost Show: Harvest Carnival of Freaks!

Thrills * Shudders * Mystery

Uncover the mysteries of the self and bear witness to
the circus of souls, the carnival of freaks, the most
heinous abominations you've ever witnessed!

Live and on-stage, ONE NIGHT ONLY!

Not To Be Missed!

Admission: 25 cents per ticket, no refunds.
Old Bierce Theatre, Corner of Hennepin & 60th Street.
Special After-Hours Screening of a Film to Follow.

"Corner of Hennepin and 60th is close. Enough time for us to make it by midnight. What say, pallies?"

"Could it really be a *real* ghost show, though?"

I caught my breath and smiled. "Now that's a question, a real fixer of a question."

We'd heard much of these legendary ghost shows growing up. They died long before our time, but as with everything in this cyclical world, perhaps they had come shambling back.

No first-hand records—no photographs, no videos, no audio recordings—existed of these macabre, nocturnal events. The evidence of their being lived on in preserved posters and in anecdotes from the older inhabitants of the city, most of whom were now dead. But stories, whispers more like, of these ghost shows, these spook shows as they were sometimes called, lived on still. Gave one the cattywumps.

They would begin with a theme: zombies, demons, asylums, the gothic. And carnivals. The audience would pay a pittance for entry. At midnight, the lights would fade and plunge the crowd from their world into that of spectacle and spiritualism. Through eloquence and cunning, the show's director, the Ghostmaster, would lure the audience into his world. The crowd would be warned about the horrors they would suffer.

With the audience so conditioned, the Ghostmaster would rely on old tricks of the Victorian spiritualist movement to summon spirits and ghoulies, and a few paid actors planted in the audience would scream, faint, add to the spectacle. Things would creep in the dark unseen; cold breath blown on the backs of frightened necks. The events would culminate in displays of depravity—a sawed off head, the spilled guts of an actor, something gruesome, a real horrorshow. And then the theatre would be plunged into darkness, and a movie would play.

Some whispers claimed that full audiences at the start of such spook shows would be slightly less so at the end, when the movie concluded and the lights came on. Some who were with their friends when the theatre went dark were *not* there when the show ended. Sometimes, those who went away did not come back.

Or was that all just part of the mystique and allure?

We hustled through the broken streets and mostly derelict buildings to make it to the theatre in time. We passed by a lit diner with large windows reminiscent of that famous painting, though the lights were dingy, the walls sodden with grease, and the customers and waitresses dead-eyed and gray as they shuffled about. The smell of bacon poured from the diner, and I was tempted to eat instead of watching this ghost show, but I was pulled along by one of my friends, and onward we went.

The theatre was a small building tucked between an abandoned warehouse with crumbling and rusted windows and a liquor store. Within that establishment the clerk moved about, dusting shelves of amber liquid. Tempted though we were to get a nip before the show, we had little time before midnight.

Marquee lights declared that Dr. Blackwood's Midnight Ghost Show—*tonight only!*—was indeed playing.

We stepped under the dim glow of the lights above the box office. I noticed pumpkins stacked into pyramids and towers surrounded by tufts of hay and grim, stuffed animals resembling crows, and remembered that it was October. Several pumpkins were carved haphazardly, lights glowing from within their fleshy recesses. It was not the aesthetic of a carnival that I expected, yet the display was more color than any of us had seen in some time. Like a candle draws moths, so did the display bring us closer.

"Four please," one of my friends said.

The box office attendant was a vague shadow in the shape of a person. They said, "One dollar."

My friend slipped four quarters across the counter, and slender fingers crept from the dark like the forelegs of a spider, grasping the coins and drawing them back into its burrow. Four tickets issued from the small hole in the plexiglass, four tattered slips of grayish paper. My friend took them and distributed one to each of us.

I stepped inside the theatre first, with my friends following me. The lobby was dim. One of the four overhead lights flickered, casting shadows over the ornate carpet. Long ago it had been scarlet with roiling curves of gold, but was now a faded, thin version of itself. There were no concessions, so we went into the theatre.

We found our seats midway to the front of the stage and sat in a clustered group. There were perhaps a dozen and a half other patrons. Nearest to us sat a couple, a woman with blond hair piled in curls and wearing a Marilyn Monroe smile. She nestled next to a man with slicked back hair and a prominent chin, who in turn wrapped an arm around her. Others sat further from us, some in the front near the stage and some within the high recesses of the back.

The stage was not decorated to resemble a carnival. There were no bright red-and-yellow tent backgrounds, no balloons.

Instead, the backdrop was that of a pumpkin patch. Several scarecrows were positioned on the stage. Their sagging, burlap heads faced us, black eyes unmoving. Tufts of straw stuck from their joints. They wore flannel, and were almost human but for their lopsided faces, where nothing was symmetrical nor drawn with care. Little pumpkins were strewn about with sloppy precision, giving the effect that the stage was the extension of the backdrop. Were we the audience meant to be the pumpkins or the scarecrows?

At the center of the stage was another scarecrow; this one was made up like a clown. Instead of flannel it wore white and red checkered pants and a silver shirt. The burlap of its face was painted white, with the large, blank eyes and lopsided face a ghastly red.

"Well," one of my friends said, his voice taut, "that at least looks a fixer of a clown, though this isn't at all like a carnival."

The clown-scarecrow stared at us.

I said, keeping my voice low, "Maybe Dr. Blackwood has changed his mind as to his theme. Maybe at midnight those pumpkins will come alive and do a circus act—trapeze, perhaps. Or better yet, the scarecrows will start juggling them like little human heads."

"All right then," the friend on my other side said. "Maybe you should go up there and put on the show, giving us the catty-wumps."

"Shh," our fourth said, "it's starting."

Somewhere, a clock struck twelve slow, deep chimes, and we four stilled in our seats as the few lights in the theatre dimmed, bringing the focus to the stage. The stifled mutterings in the audience ceased. I trained my eyes on the stage, looking at each scarecrow and pumpkin, waiting for something to move. For many stretching seconds there was no movement.

And then *he* stepped out onto the stage.

In old days they were called Ghostmasters, but this man was more like a Showman or Ringmaster. He wore a large top hat which shaded his face from the lights on the stage. Tufts of hay stuck out from the corners of the hat. He wore a long burlap coat painted deep purple, a color that seemed to both reflect and drink in the light. Staring at it turned my stomach and made me feel as though I were on a rollercoaster at the precipice of a great drop.

With skeletal white hands, he gestured at us. At first I thought he wore tight gloves, but on second glance, I could not be sure whether the hands were gloved or whether they were painted white—or if they were painted at all.

"Welcome!" he exclaimed in a scratchy voice, tilting his head upward just enough for the overhead lights to strike his chin and deep red lips, which curled into a smile showcasing yellowed teeth. "Welcome to the greatest show on earth! I am Dr. Arthur M. Blackwood, and I have come to bring you the very horrors of existence on this, the perfect autumnal evening for such things as go bump in the night."

A cool wind blew through the darkened theatre.

He continued. "I have traveled far and wide to witness the great monstrosities of our world, yes, and of other worlds! I have seen things which no mere, weak mortal can see and remain sane. And, you may ask, am I sane? I fear not, my pallies, I fear not—and after tonight, I daresay you will not be, either. Now, I promised you a carnival, a circus of freaks, and you may ask yourself—now, why do I not see a carnival?" He gestured toward us, keeping his face hidden. "Oh, but the carnival is here, the freaks are here, and a sideshow you shall see! You shall see precisely as I see, and your blood, too, shall frost over. You will beg for the safety and comfort of ignorance. But you shall not have it."

One of the scarecrows shifted. The clown-scarecrow cricked its neck, twitched an arm, then fell still again. Someone in the audience gasped.

"I have seen," The Ringmaster said, "that Great Blight, the Star Wormwood, as it shines its malevolent, green light upon the shores of crumbling Carcosa. I have seen the Great Goat of the Abyss, that which is not dead, and that which does eternal lie."

The clown-scarecrow shuffled forward on unsteady legs as

though it were a toddler. The Ringmaster put his hand up, and the scarecrow halted. The other two, each on one end of the stage, turned their heads slowly to the one in the center. I scoffed. Clearly, they were actors in scarecrow costumes.

From somewhere in the dark theatre issued a light giggling. Child-*like* and cold. The lights flickered.

"See," he said, "the greatest horror of all."

Another cold wind blew through the theatre, and I gripped the armrests of my seat as the spinning sensation of vertigo overcame me. It was as though I sat over a chasm, my chair the only thing between me and an endless fall. My companions gripped their seat so tightly that the leather armrests squeaked in protest. My vision swirled and my stomach leapt to my throat . . . and as the sensations passed, I managed to refocus on the stage. The scarecrows were moving now.

Shambling and slow, they walked toward the center. The three of them, now united, walked around the Ghostmaster, who bowed his head and lifted his white hands to the ceiling, muttering under his breath.

Suddenly, he snatched at one of the scarecrows. This was one of the ordinary ones wearing flannel. His white hands sank into the painted burlap face and squeezed, and he pulled away, tearing the head off. Tufts of hay spilled out of the thing's body cavity, yet it continued to move, swaying and shambling as it did so. As another scarecrow reached his periphery, the Ghostmaster pulled its head off as well, and then finally the clown-scarecrow's head came off. And each continued to walk. Animatronics, then, I told myself.

"Empty inside," the Ghostmaster said. "A great Nothing

made of lesser nothings."

Something skittered under our seats, something dry, and a few seconds later an audience member yelped behind us. The Ghostmaster laughed. It was deep and discordant and echoed throughout the building.

As he laughed, the three shambling scarecrows fell. They did not just sink to the stage; they fell apart totally as though every seam and stitch holding them together had been plucked loose. In floating bits of hay and fabric they fell until they were piles of autumnal refuse. A graveyard wind rolled across the theatre. It caught their clothing and innards, revealing all to be cotton stuffing, hay, burlap, and flannel. No mechanical skeleton. Empty vessels.

My hand shook as it gripped the armrest. I meant to inhale but could not. Every muscle had hitched. My chest would not expand, my lungs would not draw air, and my eyes would not shift from the pile of scarecrows I had thought, until now, were animatronic. Marionettes? But where were their strings?

"The greatest horror," the Ghostmaster said. "Dr. Blackwood has it all. He has everything for you, all you citizens of the ignorant world, deniers of the Great Truth—that of your own nonsensical nothingness. But see now!"

The theatre lights dimmed further, pressing the darkness in on us. I found my breath again, though it was shallow. Cold sweat beaded my forehead as I tried to move my wrists. I could not. Were they bound by my own psychosomatic mania, or was there something else holding them in place? This was meant to be a midnight ghost show. Smoke and mirrors and sleight of hand. The scarecrows could not have been moving on their own, had not been empty husks. Though their movement had implied life, the reality belied such a nonsense.

But it was only a show.

"Behold the spectral freakshow!"

Dr. Blackwood walked in a circle, kicking up hay and burlap until he had formed a wide circle of empty stage. From within the folds of his coat he withdrew a cane tipped with the visage of a clown with bleeding eyes. He tapped the stage, and we saw that chalk tipped the bottom of the cane. He swiped it in broad arcs, and spun on his heels and laughed as he did. All the time he kept the brim of his hat turned downward. His ghost-white fingers flexed against the dark of the wooden cane as he maneuvered it, drawing symbols within his circle. Once finished, he tossed the cane aside.

He stepped out of the circle, taking care not to smudge his chalk drawings.

"Arise," he said, his voice low at first. "I command you to arise, foul specter, true face of they who watch, arise, arise!"

Nothing happened at first, and then the light lost what little color it had. It took on a cold, blue wash. My breath fogged.

Something rose from the solidity of the wooden stage. It was transparent and made of mist, at first, and as it continued to rise the formless became formed; the colorless became, if not vibrant, an echo of color. The shape of a person coalesced from the shadows and mists and floated above the circle in the center of the stage. Its head lolled to one side. Its hands hung limply at its sides.

The head twitched, and then jerked, as if struggling to breath or align its spine. And then two grave-dark pits formed as eyes, and thin lips formed. Stringy hair sprouted from the scalp and filled in. As the face took shape and as the body formed, an uneasiness stole through my blood. I shook my head.

The familiar black hair with waves down to the neck. The nose that was neither too large nor small, but formed just above the cupid's bow of the round lips. The eyes remained blackened pits, but I did not need to see them to understand the nature of the corpse-ghost.

It was me.

But for the empty sockets where eyes should be, it was my face. The body was my height. The hands, still twitching at the thing's side, scrambling as though for air, were mine. I widened my eyes, shook my head.

"No, no . . . "

My companion was the one who spoke. And then, another friend, sitting on the other side of me, said, "It can't be—*me*." The denial came out as a whisper, choked with cold air. Around me the audience muttered. Someone else gasped.

"No." This time the voice was mine. The denial was ineffective. The hanging, glowing thing merely twitched, began clawing at its neck, the black pits of its eyes widening as though it were still choking.

"Here!" the Ghostmaster said. "The freakshow you were promised."

All a part of the show, I told myself, tricks of the magician's trade.

My corpse-ghost scratched at its face. Slowly at first, and then with ragged nails it clawed deep into the translucent skin. It reached into its eye socket voids and pulled the skin away.

As the pale skin tore away in strips, it revealed not some spectral bone or muscle, but nothing. A great, dark nothing behind its skin, and it continued to tear and rip away. Someone in the audience retched.

The dark nothing was almost a haze, something blurring the colors of this existence, smudging them out or else revealing the true reality. As skin fell away the smudge remained, vaguely human in shape, and though it turned my stomach to gaze into that void, I could not look away.

Behind the Ghostmaster, a screen descended. The lights dimmed further until we were in a sea of black.

My breath fogged and mingled with the nothing as it spread over the stage, multiplied, hovered over us. Again, something skittered under our seats, and a chill colder than ice trailed up my legs, gripped my calves.

"And now the *fun* begins," the Ghostmaster said, his voice distant, muffled. "The promised movie. Become, you wretched, sweaty things, *one of us, one of us . . .* " He repeated these words and faded into the dark. Before he was swallowed by that black chasm, though, he lifted his head into the remaining light. Through the dark-nothing haze I saw candy apple lips and a white, crumpled face and—

He was gone even as I screamed.

The lights went out. Several around me were crying. Someone was begging to be let go. Another struggled in his seat, jerking his body as though he were glued to it. I did not bother to try to escape.

Behind us, the projector came to life. On the screen, I saw not a title card but the image of a theatre with a few dozen people, staring back at us. I saw myself, haggard and gaunt. Behind me stood a shadow. On the screen, it rested a spectral hand on my shoulder, and something cold and damp pressed upon me.

On the screen, several audience members were forced out of their seats by their shadows and pulled toward the screen as though it were a giant window. Around me, several people wailed. Someone thrashed in their seat, rocking the whole row. The figure of one of the audience members was thrown at the screen, and instead of pitching through the fabric they went into it, and their double onscreen disappeared. I shut my eyes as the theatre erupted into chaos.

I kept my eyes closed even when I felt myself being pulled from my seat. As cold air pressed around me and I lost a sense of gravity, I kept them closed.

The cries, the slithering on the floor . . . all of it surrounded me as though I were in a kaleidoscope of darkness rather than color and light. Yet I kept my eyes closed, withdrew into myself, refused to look even as I felt my body thrown into some other place. All around me the screaming reached a fever pitch before leveling off into soft laughter, and then raging and cackling hysterics. How badly I wanted to open my eyes to see, but instead I curled into myself, pressed my eyes together harder—

And the yellow, misty light crept into my bedroom, and I opened my eyes. I sat up in bed, though lay back down when my stomach heaved. I could not remember getting back to my dingy apartment on the edge of the city, but the smell of sweat and alcohol clung to my pores. That and something vaguely sweeter, like carnival popcorn. My head pounded. I tried again to get out of bed, planted my feet on creaking wooden floorboards, and steadied myself as I stood. I pulled back the curtains of the small window. In the yellow, gray distance stood the towering corpse of the city. Sirens echoed through the still morning.

I rang up one of my friends. No answer. I tried the other two, and received no answer from them. Still asleep, likely. How had we stumbled from the bar to—where, the theatre?—and back to our homes? Had the Ghost Show really happened?

Doing my best to go about my day and recover from the hangover, I avoided going out. Later in the evening, I called my friends again. Only one answered, and he sounded distant and somehow lifeless, as though he was heavily drugged. I asked him if last night had really happened, and he hung up on me.

The next day one of my friends shot himself, one who had not answered on the morning after our outing. Another of our group of four disappeared the day after. Within a week the city news became obsessed with a string of suicides. And though I did not recognize the names of each, other than that of my friends, the obit pictures were familiar. The Marilyn Monroe lookalike and her partner were two of them. One of the older men who'd sat behind us. Guns, ropes, pills—the methods varied, but every few days it happened.

And now I am the only one left from that night, so far as I know, who has not leapt from a building, mixed alcohol with our city-issued tranqs, strung myself with a work tie, or taken one of the other methods detailed in the papers. I have no friends now. The last, my closest, left only a note saying he was due at Carcosa for his "birth into the void," before slitting his wrists in the bathtub.

Now I sit in my apartment staring at the crumbling monolith beyond my window, that city which seems to pulsate in the brown haze, and I wonder whether I should have opened my eyes on that long-ago night. I wonder whether the great, ruinous thing before me is any better or any worse than that which lies beyond the darkness, in the void I refused to look into. I dream about that night, about the clown-scarecrows and my own corpse-ghost, and I wake screaming and sweating.

How I now long to stare into that void.

MATHEW L. REYES is a copy editor based in the Midwest. When he's not working as an editing gremlin, he's jogging, writing, and haunting the wily, windy moors. He's had stories published with Quill & Crow Publishing, Crystal Lake Publishing, the NoSleep Podcast, and others. He is a member of the Horror Writers Association. You can find him on all socials @MathewLReyes.

WHAT DOESN'T KILL ME

Patrick Samuel

My tiger lies on the bed, eyes closed. Not asleep, just waiting on the right moment to pounce—if he can be bothered.

A yawn, a stretch of the limbs. My presence is acknowledged with the merest glance, eyebrow raised in a silent question: "What now?" I say nothing, still. One word can break the peace as surely as pebbles in a pond. Naked, he is clothed in regal disdain like a second skin. The fur has been discarded, along with any remaining pride—too hot for either.

He steps into the bathroom and after a moment I follow.

Graceful in every situation, including those involving a toilet seat. This world is his jungle, never mind the four walls and lack of space. With a snarl he conjures up darkness, the cries of exotic birds, the shape of trees and the sound of what moves behind. Hunger rules there, and the smooth run of things is merely the quiet between two storms.

Me? I bleed in silence. Where there's blood, there's life.

I USED TO have a life, as they say; and a job, and a set of rules: always make the first move, especially when it comes to leaving. Don't be needful, be needed. People called my self-assurance scary and I'd laugh.

They all thought I was crazy when I took the tiger in. Most of them alluded to the age difference, the class difference, and other differences they were too polite to mention out loud. All except Elisa, who's never read Jane Austen and thinks sense and sensibility don't apply to sisters anyway. She's been dropping hints like lead balloons lately about the importance of "staying with your own kind."

"And what kind would that be?" I ask, and get the satisfaction of her embarrassed silence.

The irony is that for once she's right on target and doesn't even know it. A pity, considering how much she'd gloat if she did. Maybe an orderly life is just a life of missed opportunities. And talking of missed opportunities, Elisa is now going on about "those great online meeting sites, so easy to make new friends."

Easy for her, maybe. She's not the one minus a breast. Given her tact I'm surprised she hasn't suggested a club for stump lovers. Apparently there's something for everyone out there. People turned on by what you lack, as if what you had wasn't enough in the first place.

I say something to that effect, despite knowing it will be lost on her.

"What doesn't kill you..." she starts again, and that's when I hang up.

WHAT DOESN'T KILL *me better run fast,* I used to say—back when my bravado felt bigger than my bra. Before what runs fast caught up with me.

Which is exactly what he did that day, as I was coming out of the doctor's office.

HE WAS DIFFERENT. Didn't pretend either but went straight for it: "Madame, you lost something," as if I'd dropped a handkerchief. It surprised me into laughter, a first since the operation.

YOUNGER. SO MUCH younger than me, some of the child still in his eyes—slightly slanted eyes on high cheekbones: sharp features under smooth golden skin. Hair black as a panther's. And the sneer, so much like him: lazy and *feral.* That should have put me on the track.

Still I was self-conscious when we undressed. His limbs were lean and hard, mine soft and pale. But he kissed the scar like a skilled lover would a place where senses meet. I felt embarrassment, relief, sharp pain—almost all at once. He didn't stop, even when the blood started running.

YESTERDAY'S EDITION OF *Le Parisien* had the story of a woman attacked on her way home. She laid on the pavement, her blouse ripped with one stroke from which blood flowed till morning. The neighbors claim they didn't hear a thing.

I believe them. I know why she didn't scream. And I know why, when she finally speaks again, she will say she doesn't remember. Once you've seen beauty, no matter how much it hurts, you don't need pity from the blind.

Before that it was a seventeen year old boy from the northern suburbs, an area so destitute that working class is considered first class. I followed up on that one, calling the hospital and pretending to be press. They don't check when you name a publication they never heard of. Either they're too busy to care or don't want to come off as totally clueless. That's how I got the boy's address. Since his release, he hasn't said a word. His family and friends still put it down to shock.

I saw him once, after a long wait outside. An older guy, possibly his brother, was carefully leading him out of the building by the arm. From where I was I couldn't see his eyes but sensed them searching furtively around and felt his sadness, deep as love requited no more.

What doesn't kill you makes you wonder if you're still alive, and whether it's worth it.

On the third night I go to sleep in my bed and wake up in the dark of another place. Stars on the ceiling, walls of leaves, a bed of damp grass. And something else, soft and warm against my body. Living, breathing fur. A paw on my naked back; the hint of a claw as I try to move. "Shhh" he goes, or the growling equivalent and I don't say a word as I feel a tongue bigger than any other, soft and raspy on my skin. I lay, heart beating against the beast that is my shelter.

THE LADY AND the tiger. Whether he's only half tiger remains debatable but I'm definitely less and less of a lady. Thirty-four, obsolete. And then there was one, and then there were none. After the ovaries came the left breast. "We might be able to save the other," said the doctor. I almost laughed. *Save it for breakfast or for remembrance?* I considered asking for a split second. When normalcy suddenly cancels its options, nothing seems too weird; not even a part-time tiger. Since my cells had decided to go crazy, why couldn't they get creative?

"You know the one about cats? Why bother giving a name to those who won't answer to it?"

"What shall I call you, then?"

He does something between a smile and a yawn, showing me his teeth. All of them.

Half a predator, half a buffoon: this is how mice must feel about the cat who comes to play.

HOW DO YOU do it? I ask another time.

What?

You know. The jungle, everything. *What's it to you,* a snarl.

It's getting to be everything but I don't say it. I've had my sick leave extended and spend the days waiting for night. I used to fear silence, now I have the scars to remind me of its virtues—and half a finger gone, from the time before we set our respective boundaries.

HIS OWN HISTORY I get in snatches too, like a corpse torn apart to be patiently reconstructed by unfazed undertakers. A word here, a sentence there. And the same shrug whenever I seek clarification. I soon learn not to ask questions; not even to myself. Sitting still and letting words come like fish in a river: memories of places, and finding the way back. The joys of blood. Species meeting their end and their new beginnings. Being what you are can be the easiest or hardest thing, depending on how you look at it.

WHY ME? THIS I know I can never ask. "I trust you," he once said in one of those fleeting moments of confidence, to be caught and treasured like rare butterflies. Trust, such an amazing word. Love without need.

I KEEP CHECKING the papers, still unsure of what I should be looking for. Cat people roaming the streets is not exactly the kind of things *Le Monde* would care to dignify in print—not in a country that prides itself on being Cartesian, the legacy of a philosopher who considered animals barely above machines and didn't mind torturing his own to prove it. Now here's one man I'd love to resurrect just to watch him die again.

Of course it is the same country that would, two centuries later, fall under the spell of terror woven by the beast of Gevaudan before succumbing to a terror even bigger, if a more human one. But as the tiger will gleefully point out, a nation that would herald the Rights of Man by slaughtering a few thousand of them shouldn't be too petty with its contradictions.

What doesn't kill you makes you see life for the joke that it is.

I WALK ALONG the banks of the Seine and picture its waters flowing red. From the French aristocrats caught up in changing times to the Algerian immigrants erased by history, the river is a fitting cemetery for a city that grew on blood but keeps pretending it was rain. And now I wonder: could the beast of Gevaudan really have been a kind of werewolf as some claimed, preying on the young and isolated, or merely a harbinger of things to come?

Maybe small sacrifices are required to stave off the big ones, I keep telling myself. Who gets to decide what is a predator, and what is a protector? I guess it all depends on where you stand in the jungle.

When the weather turns colder, I go back to mine.

"IN URBAN HUNTING, the rule is to let the prey come to you." He mimics a lecturer, the overeager narrative in a wildlife documentary. He stretches and rolls over the bed: a kitten at play, a child laughing at his own trick.

When he goofs around, I could almost believe none of this is true. Yet the truth is like that letter Poe wrote about, hidden in plain sight.

APPARENTLY THE RULE in urban hunting is to be applied. Strangers from all parts of town take to knocking on the door. Girls in their early twenties at most, boys trying to look tough; a couple I suspect to be runaways. I try to warn them in the beginning, but soon discover how hopeless it is to convince people that you are actually not mad. After a while I just nod, retreat to the bedroom. Turning pages I can't read, trying not to imagine what jungles he takes them to.

So far, no one has ever returned from them.

ONLY ONCE DID I see him relent. Axel was a drifter, in between worlds and stages of youth, with the innocence to be found fallen in the cracks. Quiet and easy-living, fair as the other was dark, even his beauty was subdued as if awaiting permission to bloom. One night the three of us sat in my living room as the walls slowly faded into another world. But I could tell something was wrong. The light, to start with: a permanent sunset bathing everything in a red glow, seductive and melancholic like a tender nightmare.

The dreamlike landscape was not of a jungle but an island from unknown tropics. I was alone; the sound of birds telling their song of times I had no part in. In the distance I saw two dark silhouettes by the water, in their own world of shadows and fiery light. A taste sweet and sour like exotic juices in my mouth as I realized Axel was taming the beast, because it had never occurred to him there was one in the first place.

I should have felt blessed to witness the miracle of miracles, the hunter captured by the game. It was a couple of weeks before I said anything. Casually, over the sink, the clang of dishes and running water: "What do you know, even tigers are human." A growl answered. *What's he been telling you?* Innocent shrug from me, half lost in the wiping of a cup. I kept my back turned, silently marveling at the predictability of predators.

If I didn't know my parents, I would swear I was the offspring of a spider and a fly. Then again, maybe there are things they never got around to telling me.

THAT NIGHT I spent locked in the bathroom, thinking I heard distant screams and sounds like branches snapping. I ran water over my hair, my ears, swollen eyes, a mouth dry as sand. Lying on the cold hard tiles, I dreamed of a sun bigger than any other burning over the red desert and a cat feeding on the remains of an antelope.

The next day we cleaned the whole place.

After that he took the hunting out of the house—at regular intervals, too, if the papers are to be believed, once you've learned to read between the lines.

I'VE LEARNED A few other things since he's been here. Like why they give names to hurricanes. How a body can be both weapon and shield. Also, that Calvin and Hobbes never had it so good. And in the little things do we find the reason for huge fucked-up trips.

HE'S BACK IN the room, hair shiny and wet. To be sure I won't break the silence unwisely, I put music on. He likes Janis, Aretha, Otis. Voices and sounds from another time and place. It's also convenient to stifle the screams.

THE LIGHT HAS changed. The music is dimming as a chorus of night birds fades in. Shapes shifting in the dark. A graze on my skin and I know it's feeding time. I open my arms; he buries his head in my chest. I am allowed to grab and cradle, and moan quietly as warm rivulets run down my side and the singing of birds swells in my ears.

THERE ARE PREDATORS and there are protectors. Small sacrifices to ward off bigger ones. And songs to remind you that love will make you bleed.

I guess that must be it then.

PATRICK SAMUEL is a French writer and translator living in Paris. His story "Southern Comfort and the Kindness of Strangers" (available in the June 2023 issue of *Prompted* magazine) was recently nominated for the 2024 Pushcart Prize. A member of the art collective Curry Vavart for several years, he is the recipient of a screenwriting grant from the Centre National du Cinéma (CNC) and currently working on several screenplays fighting to the death for his attention.

DEAR MR. SYCAMORE

Maureen O'Leary

When we were seventeen we watched *The Blair Witch Project* together at my house, do you remember? That movie scared me but you were bored the whole time and when the last scene hit, you said you would never be afraid of the woods. I'll never forget how sure you were. After the movie we snuck into my bedroom while my parents were asleep and, well, that was a nice night. We could be real quiet when we needed to be.

That was five years ago but sometimes I still chew cinnamon gum to remember the spice inside your mouth. You know why we broke up better than I do. Maybe you got sick of me. I suspected you were into another girl I never met but only heard of through other people. Her hair poured down her back like black lava and she had light brown cat eyes and cute little hips. I couldn't compete if I tried. She was one of those girls who wore flowing skirts and no makeup as if she wasn't aware of how she looked. Believe me, this girl was aware. No one has that many selfies on Instagram without knowing exactly the impact she was making. Jealousy burned in me as I scrolled her feed, leaving my insides a charred landscape. She was prettier than me, but I thought that you and I were in love and I didn't get how you could not want someone who loved you as much as I did. We were like young gods, roaring down the highway on your motorcycle at night, stopping to kiss on lonely back roads where we felt like we were the last people on the planet. When we were together no one could touch us.

I saw your new girlfriend in real life one time before. A few months after you said you didn't want to be with me anymore, I was walking around the Summer Carnival on the fairgrounds feeling sorry for myself when suddenly there you were behind the merry-go-round and you were so high your eyelids looked like they weighed ten pounds each. You were leaning into the skinny girl I recognized from her silver bangles and her glorious inky hair. I heard from people we knew in high school that you were doing real drugs even while we were dating, not just weed like you told me. As young as I was in age, I was even younger in how naïve I could be back then. I thought you liked the fact that I was so innocent. Remember when you showed up at my doorstep with a bouquet of flowers from the grocery store the summer after graduation? You told me that you would always protect me. God, I used to fantasize about marrying you. I used to think about how cute our kids would be.

When I got your letter in the mail I thought at first that someone was trolling me. Who writes letters on paper anymore? Who sends them in the mail? But you always were old-fashioned. You were the type who opened doors for me. You never let me pay for dinner. It shouldn't have seemed strange that an apology from you would come five years later in the form of a letter written in cursive on a piece of paper.

I write this letter in return with tree sap sticking between my fingers. Is this your blood on my skin? I tried washing with soap but it's still tacky. I bring my fingers to my nose and breathe you in. And now I wonder if I should explain why I came to find you when you didn't give a return address. The East Layton postmark on the envelope gave me a direction to look. You always thought that not being on social media kept people out of your business, but the diner where you were the cook has a Yelp page and you are mentioned by name as making the best biscuits and gravy in the state.

My plan was to show up at your restaurant and act like it was an accident. I was going to say that I was on a road trip through the mountains and just stopped at Friendly Jack's for something to eat. Things would unfold. You would invite me to stay the night. I imagined the taste of cinnamon gum.

Okay, let me be honest with you. I missed you. I was so lonely. And I thought if we could just see each other again, you would remember how good we were together. Maybe nothing would happen or maybe everything would. Maybe I would be so embarrassed I would want to die, but I was willing to risk looking like a fool. I would risk more than that if we could be together again. But not too much more, I guess.

The short order cook standing where I thought you were going to be said you quit weeks ago. He said you were getting high again and when I asked him where you went he said you and your girlfriend went into the backcountry and never came out and that was when I remembered that you said you would never be afraid of the woods. Then an old guy at the counter coughed into his hand and told me not to try to find you. He said that you were in the *woods* woods, not the camping woods, not the city girl woods, but the kind of woods where once you go in, you don't come out again and the cook turned his back on the both of us. I didn't order any food. I walked out with a chill up my back and the old guy followed me to my car. He pointed to the hills across the valley and he said you went where the witches live and he told me to go home.

I did not go home. The window of the East Layton Chamber of Commerce across the street had a dusty display of early settler artifacts such as a gold pan, a rusted whipsaw and a handful of square-topped iron nails from the first railroad. There were some tattered trail maps inside and the white haired lady behind the desk told me to take what I wanted. The *woods* woods outside East Layton wasn't exactly uncharted territory and I had sneakers in my car just in case you asked me to go on a hike or something.

I wondered if the ghosts of dead gold miners haunted the trail but I didn't even see another hiker. I was walking for over two hours when I found you in the clearing where the sun cooked the air so hot it was hard to breathe. I was sweaty and done with my water and thinking of that witch movie with the shaky camera and how scared I was and how unimpressed you were and I remembered the look on your face when you leaned in on that girl at the Summer Carnival, as though she had the only thing you needed in the entire world to be happy. You didn't see her turn her head and look at me as if she knew exactly who I was and almost like she expected me to be there. Her eyes narrowed over her big teeth grin and a terrible sickness gripped my entire body. The Summer Carnival was crowded with people on dates, and little kids, and packs of teenagers, but I felt like an intruder when I happened upon the two of you. I felt like I didn't belong there, like I didn't belong anywhere. My stomach heaved into my throat and I ran until I hit the parking lot where I puked behind somebody's truck. I never saw you again, like I said, but I heard you went deeper into drugs. I heard your girlfriend was a witch, like a real one. I couldn't worry about you too much however because I had a wave of my own bad luck to deal with. The next day my manager at the bookstore accused me of stealing off the shelves and I lost my job. A strange rash popped up around my lips and inside my mouth that made eating anything but vanilla pudding very painful and no doctor could find medicine that worked to cure me. When the rash finally went away, I found that every time I bit into a piece of fruit in those days, an earwig crawled out of it. It wasn't for over a year until my life was set right again.

So maybe you won't be surprised that looking for you in the woods today I was afraid. What was I afraid of? I was afraid of bears. I know that only black bears live in the Sierra and that they don't attack people unless they are provoked. You are the one who taught me that. You are also the one who taught me to trust the hairs on the back of my neck standing up as a sign of real danger. You are the one who taught me that if you take away the highways and the malls and the screens and the noise, humans are ancient beings not far under the surface. I was afraid of ancient beings. I was afraid of your girlfriend.

In your letter you said, *I make amends for hurting you. You were always too good for me. I wanted to be the nice guy you thought I was but that wasn't me. I had a choice between an angel and a devil and I went for the devil. Some guys deserve to be blessed and some guys deserve to be cursed. We know which one I am but you best believe I did not want you to get caught up in my mess.*

There were a few sentences about how you had a straight job. You were trying meetings to get sober. *Lately I catch myself thinking of you. And I know before anything else happens, I have to get right with you and say I am sorry. I hope you accept this apology from my deepest heart.*

I stuck my finger into my back pocket to feel your letter folded there and then I saw you. The air itself was dense and quiet. You were bent over muttering to the girl from the Summer Carnival, the one with the serpentine face and amber-colored eyes. She was pretty like some girls are, so pretty she makes you feel hopeless. She didn't look at me that time but I saw her touch your cheek and walk into the trees though there was no snapping of twigs under her sandals.

The smell of woodsmoke perfumed your letter and you wrote in that rounded printing I would know anywhere. You said you were sorry but I forgave you already, don't you know that? Don't you remember the nights in the park when we lay on our backs in the grass and looked at the stars and told each other stories of witches and princes and faery queens? I guess you were high back then but in a way so was I. I was high on first love. I was high on you kissing me so hard I got dizzy in the best way. I read something online that first love makes a mark on a person that never goes away. I guess I felt I had a right to come find you. We were each other's first everything. I didn't take the letter as an invitation, but I did take it as proof of ownership. You owned me in ways I still can't explain and I thought this would be a story we could tell our kids and grandkids. Dad was sick for a while, but then he got well and Mama loved him so much she hiked into the woods alone to find him.

The black-haired girl was gone in a flash of silver so quick that I thought she was a trick of my dehydrated brain. I called your name. You were standing still with your back curved as if you carried a heavy load across your shoulders. My voice was flat in the clearing as if we were in a room with walls made of trees. You turned to see me finding you, and the sound your body made was wood twisting in on itself, a private sound between the trees.

I knew it was you. I knew you even though your face was so gaunt that your cheeks caved in and your eyes sank so far beneath your brow that I couldn't say for sure if I actually saw them glinting in the sunbeam filtering through the leafy canopy or if I just remembered how improbably green they were when I first met you outside American Lit class when we were in high school. By the time I crossed the clearing your skin was hardened into gray and white bark and your arms were outstretched in glorious branches.

From behind the trees I thought I heard a woman laughing. I pressed my nose into your trunk and smelled cinnamon and wood-smoke and I wanted to weep for you but instead I left you there alone because though I sign this now with all of my love, this is my way of saying goodbye forever because I *am* afraid of the woods.

MAUREEN O'LEARY is a California writer. Her work has appeared in *Bourbon Penn, Nightmare, Creepy Podcast, Tales to Terrify, Tahoma Literary Review, Punk Noir, Dark Winter Lit* and other places. She is a graduate of Ashland MFA.

READING SLOANE

Jason A. Wyckoff

Althea arrived five minutes before the appointed hour despite knowing full well her sister was sure to be ten minutes late. There seemed little chance of drawing the ire of the two friendly young people on staff, as there were plenty of open seats in the café; still, she preferred to wait with a coffee in hand, and so placed her order immediately upon arrival. On a whim, she splurged and got herself a white chocolate raspberry latte. She sat at a tall, round 'two-top,' wood painted blue, near a window. She tucked her feet onto the stool's footrest and leaned forward; her fingers framed a triangle around the scalloped base of her glass. She breathed in the enjoyably cloying scent. Her glasses fogged and she stuffed them in the pocket of her sweater.

The café was the sort to flaunt its independent ownership through eclecticism. An exhibit of cartoonish surrealism hung from the walls, small works in repurposed frames. The service bar, shelves, and molding were classic walnut, inherited from the previous owner; but otherwise, none of the furniture matched. Sloane would probably want to move to one of the sofas when she arrived; Althea gazed at a lime-green couch and the battered box of a checkers set on a crate in front of it as though fated to join them. But she lingered where she was, gazing out the window. The snow was snow again; sparse, fat flakes fell on a deceitful slurry of grey slush and ice. Traffic crawled; spinning tires hissed to inch forward.

The bell on the door clanked hard in protest. Sloane cursed as she kicked her boots against the door frame and shook moisture from an uncovered tangle of curls down onto her shoulders. Wet suede chilled Althea's chin as she stretched to hug her sister.

Sloane glanced once at the table and then instructed, "Why don't you go grab that couch? It'll be warmer. Fuck this weather." She waved at a swollen loveseat upholstered in blonde mohair at the far end away from the windows. "What the hell is that?" She nodded at Althea's drink.

"An indulgence," Althea said.

Sloane snorted. "Jesus. Whole damn world's gone topsy-turvy."

Althea grabbed her coat from her chair and moved to the

requested seat while Sloane waited at the counter for a black coffee with two shots of espresso.

Sloane indicated the latte when she sat. "I would've got that for you."

Althea shook her head slightly. "That's not necessary."

Sloane slumped dramatically. "I know, I'm an ass. I didn't even ask you if you had an appointment."

"No. Nothing 'til later." This was true, but only coincidentally. Althea had had a lunchtime appointment scheduled, but Mrs. Hutchins texted to cancel on account of the weather right before Althea was going to phone to tell her something had come up.

"I'm sorry, I'm just . . . " Sloane jutted out her lower jaw and rolled her eyes up, revealing crescents of crimson-tinged white over black eyeliner. "I feel like my head's going to burst. My life is falling apart."

It was nothing Althea hadn't heard before. This was fairly standard language for a 'Sloane'-level emergency. Althea never begrudged her the frequency of such seemingly dire circumstances. If venting alleviated her sister's stress, Althea was happy to accommodate her. Subsequently, the passage of a few days usually mitigated the crisis. Althea would remind her sister of this, as sensitively as possible, on those rare occasions when Sloane would push for something more than 'normal' insight or advice.

Althea soon became wary that this was going to be just such an occasion. Sloane was caught in a four-wind storm: health, home, work, and romance. The last was, as usual, the precipitating event for the sisterly confab. Yes, she *knows* she'd only been out with Zachary a few times (Althea knew 'going out a few times' unquestionably entailed sex) and no, they'd never *said* they were exclusive (and under different circumstances, it might have been Sloane who kept things deliberately vague) but she really thought he might be the one, and he was such a dick about it when she found out that they weren't, saying how he couldn't understand why she was so upset. Maybe if he'd been honest from the beginning they could move past it; as it was, they were over; she couldn't stand to see his face again. And now she had no one, and she didn't know anyone, and she would have to start all over again with someone who was going to just turn out to be another loser, anyway.

"You've never had any problems attracting men," Althea pointed out.

"Always the wrong kind, though!" Sloane replied. Althea didn't have to look to know a few heads had turned at the volume of the proclamation. "I don't think I'll ever be in a good relationship. Perhaps we're doomed because we lost the most decent man we'll ever know too young," meaning their father.

Althea didn't react to the equation of her one significant relationship and subsequent divorce with Sloane's restless bed-hopping. It was curiously reassuring in a misguided way, with its back-handed tenderness. But it was the follow-up which bothered her.

"Poor Dad," Sloane said. "Poor Gran."

Leaving their mother out didn't surprise Althea; she and Sloane were permanently estranged at this point. The rapprochement between mother and daughter which usually followed the tumultuous teen years never came for the two of them. But pairing their father with their grandmother alluded to why *she* should be pitied in relation to his demise, and that intimated something else.

Their Dad was Gran's son-in-law, but she grew to love him as much as her own flesh and blood, and, perhaps because their relationship was unfettered by history and familial squabbles, she loved him with an unreserved and buoyant joy that was for him alone. At a gathering during Althea's second Christmas break back from college (with Sloane a senior in high school, yearning to break free), her Dad's brother, their Uncle Mike, presented him with a gift in a tall, red bag. Anyone could guess it held a bottle. Dad rarely drank, but he would enjoy a tumbler of bourbon with water in quiet moments. He shouted, "Hey-hey!" in appreciation when he drew the bottle from the bag. Gran was behind him and asked, "What is it?"

He turned around and presented the bottle of Maker's Mark. Gran screamed and collapsed. She'd read the drip of red wax on the bottle's neck.

Everyone knew Gran's power. They all knew she'd seen something terrible. After she'd revived, she tried to reassure them, that, no, she was just startled, she read the sign incorrectly; but her shaking voice and her eyes, darting towards and then away again in horror from the whiskey bottle, betrayed her. And the way she favored Dad, patting him, reassuring *him* especially, made the subject of the fortune painfully obvious.

Dad laughed it off. But he, too, believed. Gran could never have got on with him so well if he'd thought she was a superstitious kook. Still, he kept a brave face. Through the force of his convivial determination and his earnest invocations of the magic of Christmas, he almost made everyone believe things would be all right.

Gran knew better. Gran knew dad couldn't escape his fate. But because she loved him as she did, she tried anyway. She was a fortune teller because divination of the future was a family talent that was, for them, real and quantifiable. Wards and charms were for the rubes. Nevertheless, her hopes turned to the esoteric—or as she had previously held, the fraudulent. She enlisted her daughter's aid; blue concentrically-circled Turkish evil eyes were hung on every window sash; bundles of pungent herbs tied in the shape of a man found their way under Dad's pillow—to his consternation. He balked, ineffectively, at the laying on of polished stones.

Had it been any other disease, early detection following from prognostication would likely have been a great asset. Unfortunately, there was no medical treatment any more effective than Gran's wards and charms for Dad's rapidly progressing pulmonary alveolar microlithiasis. In the end, it only brought a longer period of worry before Dad began to cough and his lungs turned to stone.

It was a terrible time for the whole family, of course. It was horrible for the sisters to lose their father; horrible to have to lose him like *that.* Sloane reacted badly. She refused to accept the inevitable. She wanted to fight. With no direct foe available, she lashed out at their mother. Althea thought that, despite every maternal instinct, her mother truly did hate Sloane at times for her selfishness during that period. All the while, Althea's talent was burgeoning, but seeing how much pain it brought her Gran, she did her best to hide it. The bloom of foretelling the future seemed like the very definition of adding insult to injury. Especially as Gran's anxiety about Dad caused a sympathetic withering and deterioration to her own health, while her search for a silver bullet depleted her savings and caused her to neglect her customers. Dad couldn't help but get frustrated trying to protect Gran from making choices which hurt her. In the end, their contending noble sentiments only served to strain their relationship in the last months of his life. And, as he correctly predicted, without any latent talent, Gran never recovered from the tribulation of that time, and she herself passed just four years later.

In the interim she had made Althea promise nevermore to read family. Althea reminded Sloane repeatedly of that rule, but it never stopped her sister from trying. Bringing up the inspiration for exactly why she wouldn't do it seemed an unlikely gambit to elicit a reading, but Sloane's second move put it in context: Having started with the worst thing that could happen, she then contrasted it with the best.

"Christ," she said. "Gran versus the tornado. Do you remember that?"

"Who could forget?" No one could; it was impossible.

When they were younger, Gran lived on a country road near Groveport, Ohio, just outside of Columbus and very nearly at the acute northeastern tip of the great swath of country colloquially known as 'Tornado Alley.' Late one summer afternoon when her family was visiting, the western sky turned slate grey, wriggling with tinges of sickly green. The wind began to whistle through the eaves of Gran's house. Black clouds loomed and rolled like a trample of hooves. Thunder nearly drowned out the sirens. Everyone rushed to the basement. Except Gran. She went out the front door. Dad ran after her, but she waved him back inside no matter how much he protested. She went over to the neighbors' house, collected the family of five, and marched them back to her place. Why did they come? Because they believed her when she said they would be safe. Everyone huddled against the stone walls of the cellar. Except Gran. She sat at the top of the stairs and smoked a cigarette.

The neighbors' house was leveled. She told them, "I'm sorry, I didn't know your house was going to be destroyed. I just knew this one wasn't." They thanked her for keeping them alive.

"How did she know?" Sloane asked. "She never did say."

"She told me." Of course she did. Because of the gift they shared, her Gran had told her how she saw it, and her sister had likely guessed that. "Don't you remember what she was doing earlier that day?"

"I remember we were laughing at her because she was out staring at the road."

"That's right," Althea confirmed. "She'd seen the forecast and she knew the danger. She was re-reading the sign just to be sure. She read it in the script of tar the road crew had left patching the cracks in the asphalt. It said, 'This house will stand another seventy years.' "

Sloane laughed. "You're serious? Tar writing? But why wouldn't she tell us?"

"Because it was so serious. There's no great risk in believing tea leaves foretell a baby boy in the coming year. But try putting your faith in a sign when the stakes are that high. Even believing in her gift, even benefiting from the outcome, Mom and Dad would have been appalled to know she strolled out into a tornado based on a thing like that."

"Well, they would have been wrong." Sloane's gaze drifted far away as she held her coffee under her nose. "Do you remember the catalpa tree?"

She was really working the angles. From the worst to the best to sentimentality for childhood games. They used to pluck flowers from Gran's catalpa tree and take them to her to read. She would make a show of pulling down the 'tongue' of the white trumpet to read the magenta dots and lines inscribed inside. Althea wondered what she might have really seen. Telling a child's fortune was not difficult: "You're going to have chicken pot pie for dinner tomorrow!" "You're going to fall and scrape your knee the next time you roller skate!" In autumn, when the orb weavers crowded near the house, she would read their zigzag signatures and tease the girls by telling them which boys liked them and give them hints of as-yet-unconsidered Christmas gifts.

"I'm not going to read you," Althea said quietly but firmly.

Sloane sputtered with mock exasperation. "I wasn't going to ask you to!" She shook her head indignantly. "Though really, I don't think a *flower's-worth* is too much to hope for, with all I've got going on!"

And so followed the rest. On Sloane's last visit to the dentist, he'd advised her that the partially-impacted tooth which bothered her from time-to-time definitely *had* to be extracted, and soon; she had the insurance to cover the procedure now, but maybe for not much longer: she dreaded going in to work anymore, as the mega-corporation her now-comfortably-retired former boss had sold his company to ran their finance arm through a call center halfway around the world, and her hag of a new boss hated her, besides; and she couldn't relax at home, between the hammer-and-anvil pinging of her useless radiator and the incessant wailing of the newborn downstairs.

As Sloane listed her various misfortunes, Althea silently thanked the changing times for the city-wide smoking ban. Despite all her practice at 'blurring the eyes of her mind,' it was too easy to read the whorls; such a personal thing, coming out from the inside. She used to have to look away from her sister while she spoke, which invariably led to an accusation that she wasn't even listening. But she always listened; she always cared.

"Thank God I never even *wanted* children," Sloane said, and she began to lean forward and stretch out her arm, as if she forgot she did not hold a cigarette to extinguish.

It was an absentmindedly cruel thing to say. Althea had a son, Jonathan. Her marriage collapsed and her husband left when Jonathan was four years old. They shared custody, but he moved away a year later. For almost a decade, she and her son formed a contented and self-sufficient pair. But as Jonathan got older, the taunts from boys about how his mother earned her living hooked deeper. Inevitably, he started to worry what *girls* would think of it. And then there was the reality of her gift: it wasn't telepathy, but it was near enough to a terrified teenage boy who craved privacy. She tried to reassure him that she would never read him, but how could he believe it—when she didn't have anything *else* in her life to care about? Shortly after he turned fourteen, he asked if he could go live with his Dad. Althea was shocked that her ex-husband assented.

She couldn't read anything beyond the text of his messages, but she thought the choice was endorsed (or demanded) by his second wife, who seemed to burn with the strange jealousy some victors feel towards the vanquished.

"I'm sorry, that was a stupid thing to say," Sloane sighed. Althea was surprised by the apology. She'd learned year upon year to control her reactions, so as to never betray her feelings, lest she read something for one of her clients that should be left unsaid. Perhaps her sister could read Althea's silence better than she thought. She made a mental note to consider what she communicated when she did not respond.

"Don't worry about it," she said.

"Is Jonathan doing okay?"

Althea didn't know. "He's doing okay."

"Well, hey, at least I can do one thing right today." Sloane reached into her bag and pulled out a paperback book which she sat on the seat between them. "Here, you can have this back." It was a mystery novel by Louise Penny which Sloane had borrowed from Althea 'to have something to read on the plane.' The trip had been aborted, and Sloane had had the book for the six months since. Althea never expected her to return it. There was a receipt used as a bookmark halfway through the book. Althea knew it didn't indicate where Sloane had stopped reading (if she'd read any of the book at all). It had been placed with deliberate haphazardness.

Althea was a good fortune teller, but she couldn't read nearly every 'random pattern' the way Gran had been able to (Gran once weaved around the main atrium of the City Center Mall like a drunkard for ten minutes after she caught sight of a piece of fractal art). It was clear Althea had the generation-skipping gift, but it took the two of them years of working together to understand exactly what she was capable of (training which Althea was somewhat disinclined towards, as she could see how it distanced her from her sister). Althea could only read inanimate things that a subject had touched. She didn't use Tarot cards, because too many impressions lingered, and her reading likely would stray from the 'established' interpretation, which a knowledgeable student might recognize. She could read tea leaves if requested to, but she preferred a method she'd discovered for herself: she would have a client 'concentrate on the question' (it wasn't necessary for the reading, but it promoted the client's sense of investment in the process) as they drew liquid in a dropper from a vial of food-coloring. She would then ask that they 'release' the question as they pushed the plume of color into a large, clear beaker of water. They were welcome to use up to three colors of their choosing, though usually everything Althea needed to see she could read as the first ringlets unwound. One of her less-often used techniques, but one which was also very effective, and one which Sloane was well aware of, was to read the little rivers between words on a printed page, the vein-like lattices similar to crown shyness in a tree canopy. The cramped print of 'pocket' paperbacks condensed these background patterns, and a slight relaxing of focus washed them into clear relief, easily read.

"Thanks," Althea said. "I'd forgotten about it." She grabbed the paperback off the seat and moved it across her lap, putting it straight into her bag without further consideration.

Sloane sighed with frustration. She picked at her cuticles

and bounced one knee. "You've been given a *gift*," she said with a hint of bitterness, meant to point out the imbalance between them; Sloane had no such talent.

"It has its limitations," Althea said, referencing the fact that she could not read for herself, and therefore not reading for her sister actually put them on equal footing in that regard. "And it can't change anything."

"I know that!" Sloane cried. "I can make my own change. I've *always* gone my own way. I just need a little hope to get me through. Somehow!"

She stopped scratching, and she stilled her knee. Her shoulders slumped. She said, "Do you ever worry that you're *not* about to reach your limit? Like, you feel so overwhelmed by the weight and the pressure of your life, and you think, 'if just one more thing goes wrong, I'll break.' And you know that if that happens, everything—*everything*—will fall apart and you'll lose what little you have, but—but maybe then you can leave it all behind, and you'll be broken, but you'll be free—free for real change, for something new? But you know the truth is you *won't* break; that 'one more thing' will be just one more thing that you carry, and you *will* go on, teased by that collapse just out of reach, suffering, without relief, just because you're strong enough to keep going, and not smart enough to know how to stop."

Sloane sniffled and rubbed one eye with the heel of her palm. "Goddammit," she hissed. "Look, I've got to go to the bathroom, and then I'd better get back to work." She launched out of her seat and snatched up her coat.

Althea patted the air. "Just leave your stuff and come back.

I'll watch it."

"Fine." Sloane threw her coat down and stormed off, unmindful of the patrons watching her as she passed.

Maybe this time it *was* worse than usual. Sloane might lament the various injustices the conspiring universe allayed against her quite vocally at times, but it was unlike her to be 'maudlin' or to 'show weakness' (as she would see it). Althea knew the truth was neither of their lives was much to crow about, but she took comfort that at least they had each other. It could be exhausting to be the stolid, quiet one, the much-abused sounding board, but Sloane was strong in her way, and Althea drew strength from her sister's ability to endure—even if, as the quiet one, she wasn't the sort to tell her sister that she found her so inspiring (it wasn't easy to work it into their conversations: 'My life is trash.' 'You inspire me!').

Althea pulled the paperback from her bag and opened to the bookmarked page. She blurred her eyes a bit and read the empty squiggles.

Then she closed the book and put it back in her bag and waited for her sister to return.

She mustn't think too much about it.

She had practiced half her life how to not say things. She had practiced half her life how to not betray what she was feeling. In truth, she'd been doing both long before she suspected her talent.

She finished her latte.

Sloane came back for her coat, just as hot as when she'd left. When she bent to grab it, Althea reached over and put her hand on her sister's wrist.

"What?" Sloane asked.

"You know that I love you."

"Yeah, okay."

Althea kept her hand where it was.

"What?"

"You're not leaving until you say you love me, too."

Sloane was flummoxed. She looked at her sister's smile. It was beatific, as always.

She snickered. *"Okay.* I love you, too. Nerd."

"Was that so hard?"

Sloane laughed. Althea stood and they embraced.

As they were putting their coats on, Althea said, "You know, it's not all bad to not read your family. The great joy of my life is not knowing how Jonathan is going to turn out, to not know what kind of man he's going to become—and yet, being absolutely certain of how proud I'll be. I'm never happier than when I'm wondering about that."

"Wondering, huh? Still seems overrated to me."

Outside, the snow was falling more heavily. Althea put on her knit hat.

"Where'd you park?" Sloane asked.

"I took the bus. I don't like to drive in the snow."

"The bus? Shit, I wish we'd left a few minutes ago, I could have run you home." Sloane frowned, looking at the traffic. "Screw it. I'll take you, anyway. Maybe I'll get lucky and my bitch boss will fire me."

"No," Althea said. "Don't worry about me. And hey." She grabbed her sister's hands and held them. "You are the strongest person I know. I don't need to read your future to know that you can endure anything life throws at you."

Sloane tried to smile; it came out crooked. "Awesome. But you're still not going to give me anything, are you?"

Althea thought for a second, tried to suppress a grin, and then sputtered into a quick giggling fit.

"Oh my God, what?"

"You're going to reconcile with Mom."

Sloane's jaw dropped and her eyes popped. And then she laughed. "You're such a dick." She started away, waving back. "And you've *clearly* lost your gift."

Althea stood at the bus stop for almost twenty minutes. She bounced on the balls of her feet and hugged herself to keep warm. A man kicking through the slush as he passed by called to her, "Not a good day for the bus to be late, is it?" She smiled and shrugged. "What can you do?"

Finally, she got on and sat near the front. She put her bag on her lap and cradled it.

She wondered if Jonathan would have children. She wondered if he would have a baby girl. Would she have the gift? It would be hard on her, without anyone to teach her and to warn her about the pitfalls. It would be hard on Jonathan, afraid for his baby to have to go through something he'd never understood or wanted any part of.

Althea couldn't read herself. But it was the easiest thing to read when someone was about to lose a beloved sister.

The bus turned away from the downtown area. It fishtailed briefly as it merged onto the divided road heading towards the bridge, but the driver was undeterred and continued to accelerate, trying to make up for lost time.

JASON A. WYCKOFF is the author of two short story collections published by Tartarus Press, *Black Horse and Other Strange Stories* (2012) and *The Hidden Back Room* (2016). His short stories have also appeared in numerous anthologies and journals. His first novel, IXIXIKLIS, is due out in October from Grendel Press. He is fated never to leave Columbus, Ohio. Married, with cats.

FURTHER READING

If you enjoyed this publication, be sure to check out the many other projects available under the Chthonic Matter imprint:

Nightscript
An 8-Volume Anthology

Twice-Told
A Collection of Doubles

Oculus Sinister
An Anthology of Ocular Horror

Come October
An Anthology of Autumnal Horror

Tenebrous Antiquities
An Anthology of Historical Horror

ABOUT THE EDITOR

C.M. Muller lives in St. Paul, Minnesota with his wife and two sons—and, of course, all those quaint and curious volumes of forgotten lore. He is related to the Norwegian writer Jonas Lie and draws much inspiration from that scrivener of old. His tales have appeared in *Shadows & Tall Trees, Dim Shores, Vastarien,* and a host of other venues. He has published two collections of his short fiction: *Hidden Folk* (2018) and *Secondary Roads* (2022).

www.chthonicmatter.wordpress.com